The

WALRUS

in the

COFFIN

M Findlay

ISBN: 9798708006769

Chapter One

There are indeed more things in heaven and earth than many could dream of, and there are those of us that do in fact dream of just such things. One person who's mind is cast in such a way is Professor Thorebourne - my benefactor and surrogate family. It is he that first dreamt of such an impossible invention that none other have since conceived of (as far as I'm aware). I will tell about this as best I can, although I have doubts as to whether any would believe me.

I imagine anyone listening to my tale would quickly dismiss such ramblings as those of a wandering mind or spinner of falsehoods. I wouldn't blame them of course. Even to my own ears it still seems fanciful and rather far-fetched. I can scarcely believe it happened myself.

I hardly know where to start, but in the very best traditions of story telling, the beginning seems as good a place as any, at least at the beginning of my involvement in such an extraordinary tale at any event. I should begin by telling a little of myself, and considerably more of Professor Wendell Thorebourne, the instigator and lead protagonist in my story.

In the year 1861, the very same year that our queen lost her beloved husband, Albert, I was taken in by a gentleman of science. Professor Thorebourne is a wealthy man, and it was a surprise to me to find myself being introduced to a serious yet kindly looking man one sunny September afternoon. I'd resided at the orphanage ever since my father had been killed fighting in the Crimea eight years previous. My mother fell ill shortly after receiving word of his death and my siblings and I found ourselves in an orphanage with no one else to care for us. To this day I know not of where my two brothers and sister are, being only two years old when I accompanied them to the orphanage. I can only hope that they are well, and living their lives in a similar comfort to that of which I've become accustomed to.

As I was led into the Master's office that fateful day, I was sure that I had somehow transgressed the rules and thoroughly expected a beating at the very least. I can still remember the ticking of the clock that stood in the hallway outside, and as the matron led me into his room and closed the door, the ticking could no longer be heard. It was as if the room itself were holding its breath in anticipation of my fate. I was surprised to see a well dressed man, a cane in one hand and top hat in the other, standing in front of the master who was a rather severe man at the best of times. He turned his balding head to look at me with a scowl that I was sure was permanently etched upon his features, and grimaced. I recall the somewhat shocked realisation that this was in fact an attempt at a smile, the first one I'd ever witnessed from him, and one that seemed to fail dismally.

The unknown gentleman smiled down at me as I stood nervously by the door, wondering what this meant and never once considering that such a person would ever take me away from such a grim existence, although I confess, I know not of whether I judged my life at the orphanage in such an unkindly way at the time, having never known anything else for the past

3

eight years of my young life.

'This is Professor Thorebourne, young William. He is to be your benefactor, and you will be taking your leave of our establishment in order to make your way in the world.' The Master said, puffing out his chest importantly. 'Well, what have you to say to that, Boy?'

I don't think I quite understood what was happening at this point in the proceedings, as all I could do was stare at the Professor's silver fob chain as it glinted in the late afternoon sunlight as it streamed through the window, half blinding me.

'Are you quite sure you want this particular boy, Professor? We have a number of bigger and stronger boys that would acquit themselves most well in any work you may require from them.'

'Oh, yes, Sir,' I stared up at the professor as he smiled warmly, first at the master and then at me. 'If he has as keen a mind as you say, he'll be perfect. It'll be a life of science and discovery that awaits him. A life of meaning that will require intelligence and wits. I have no need of a strong back, or at least, none so pressing.' This was the first time I witnessed one of the Professor's jaunts into another world, where he would mentally depart the existence which he shared with other men and transcend into an altogether higher plain of thought. He looked about the room without seeing for several seconds as all those present waited for the promise of his verbal conclusion. 'No, No, I'm quite sure.' He continued all of a sudden, his brow softening and his eyes refocusing on his surroundings as if with a start. 'It is a companion I require. One to document and assist in my work. Young William here will do quite nicely, I believe.'

And that was that. There was some paperwork involved I recall, but my attention was firmly fixed on this enigma of a man as I watched him conclude his business with the orphanage, before I was allowed to collect what little possessions I had and follow him through the gates of the institute that had been my home for so long.

For the first few weeks I lived in a state of permanent disbelief. The ride in his carriage took forever to a ten-year old boy, but eventually we arrived at a large house on the very outskirts of London that I would soon come to think of as home. We were on the very western fringes of the city, and there was little to see beyond the grounds other than fields and a distant church spire. A large brick outbuilding stood at the rear of the main property, which was a magnificent looking three story house. It was a revelation to be free of the bustling, filthy streets of the inner city.

My education commenced almost immediately, and I suspect I fell somewhat short of my benefactor's expectations. Nonetheless, he treated me patiently and between bouts of his own work he continued to further my knowledge of the world. In particular I was taught to read and write to a much higher standard. Mathematics was a particular favourite of his, but everything paled into comparison to the physical sciences. I was soon being furnished with such tomes as Auguste de La Rive's "Treatise on Electricity", and Fleeming Jenkin's "Electricity and Magnetism". 'Essential pre-reading in preparation for our work', he explained in all seriousness as he handed me this last work, just one day into my fifteenth year.

I was perfectly aware as my studies progressed that a great works was underway within the outbuilding. As tall as the main house, and cavernous on the inside with an impressively curved roof above, it was simply referred to as "the barn", but it remained largely out of bounds to me until I turned eighteen years. There were many comings and goings over the preceding years. Workmen would spend days or weeks at a time, behind closed doors (and they were enormous doors) hammering and such, bringing in large pieces of metalwork and wood. My curiosity grew steadily, yet the professor insisted that it was too dangerous to enter as yet. I gave him my word to respect his wishes until the time came that my involvement would be required.

The professor himself had his usual workshop in the basement of the house, and I would often visit with him there, marvelling at the curious array of scientific apparatus and fancy contraptions, the use of which I had little idea. The professor was often deep in contemplation, and at times it was difficult to extract a response to my questions born out of a natural curiosity. At other times he was most enthusiastic to explain the meaning or use of a particular piece of equipment or invention, so much so that I often lost track of his explanation as he spoke of things that I had little knowledge of at that time.

One day, he began to explain his theory on a newly created piece of equipment, offering perhaps my first insight into what was to lie ahead of us both.

'Magnetism, my boy! That's the thing, you understand. The key is to create a magnetic field of such proportions that you can attract and hold the very particles of existence located in another place entirely. It's just a case of creating and controlling a powerful enough field.' He wandered off into that higher plain for a while then, mumbling incoherently, his eyes widened every so often as his mind connected another piece of the puzzle. As always I let him go, waiting for that inevitable moment that he would return to me, his gaze drifting about the room for a while before focusing back upon myself, that enigmatic smile spreading across his lips once more. 'Won't be long now, William, you'll see. My, my, indeed you will.'

I didn't know then just how close he was to his breakthrough, or indeed just how incredible and tragic our journey was to become.

6

Chapter Two

That first morning when I was so ignominiously shaken from my slumber, I thought the world was falling in upon itself. I can remember opening my eyes as I became aware of being shaken, and I expected to see the professor before me, waking me amidst one of his eureka moments that would happen on occasion. When no one came into view, I struggled toward full wakefulness, aware of the shaking becoming ever more apparent.

I laid there initially, gripping the sheets as if they would protect me against whatever upheaval were assaulting the room about me, but eventually I rolled from my bed and laid upon the floor, trying to make sense of such a vibration coursing through my world. Seeing that I remained unhurt, and fearing for the professor, I swiftly pulled on some clothing before making my way from the room.

It was soon apparent that the movements were not so violent as to endanger the building itself, yet a fearful whine could be heard at the back of the house. A sound that I'd never heard before and could not account for in any logical way. The door to the professor's bedroom was open, and I quickly cast my eyes around it, confirming that he was nowhere to be seen. I then staggered my way down the stairs, holding on as I tried desperately to imagine what the source of such a disturbance could possibly be.

At first I headed toward the basement door, increasingly certain that it must be related to one of the Professor's experiments, but it was soon apparent that the frightful noise was coming from somewhere outside - from the direction of the barn. As I reached the door in the back of the house, I pulled it open, standing on the threshold as I looked to where I knew the noise and vibrations were emanating from. It could only mean one thing. That whatever was in there. Whatever the professor had been building over the past few years, was now in operation.

I admit, it took a certain amount of thought before I found the courage to leave the house and head toward the barn. My promise to never enter the outbuilding until the professor had requested I do so ran through my mind, but there seemed little point to such a promise now. I could hardly be expected to ignore such a thing, and the idea that something may have gone wrong. That the professor may indeed have been injured, drove me out into the grounds and toward the source.

I could feel the vibrations through my feet as I walked swiftly along. It was a most disconcerting sensation. As I reached the barn, the sound had increased in pitch and I was forced to cover my ears with my hands. Faced with a closed door, I had little choice but to drop my guard in order to push it open, and then, as I bravely stepped inside, I was immediately assaulted with the most horrendous sound. My hands did little to protect me as I stared about me, seeing a monstrous machine that had been built within. Steam was spewing outward, partially obscuring the sight of a large metal wheel of sorts spinning around at a tremendous rate. This was undoubtedly the cause of the vibrations, and indeed the noise that was making rational thought all but impossible. I stared in wonder for a time before catching sight of the professor, waving his arms frantically at me to leave. Unlike me he wore some kind of muffs about his ears and a pair of goggles over his eyes. In an almost stupefied state, I backed out of the building and retreated enough that I could once again regain a level of clearheadedness.

There was a distinct change in the noise levels, and then the vibrations began to diminish. As the sound slowly wound itself down I realised the machine had been turned off, and that the professor was now approaching me. I thought he would be angry with me but his face bore an expression of delight, and possibly a little concern for myself.

'My boy, it's working. It's working, my boy,' he said, grinning like a madman.

'I didn't know what it was,' I explained, determined to offer my reasons for invading his domain. 'I felt the vibrations, and then the noise! Professor, the noise!' I realised I was speaking rather loudly at this point. Somewhat louder than would be normal, even when outdoors.

'My boy, you should've worn something about your ears, it can be rather loud in there,' he said, somewhat unnecessarily I thought. 'Come, let me show you. It's perfectly safe now. As you can tell, it's running down. The important thing is that it works, my boy, it works!'

I stood for a moment as the professor turned away, feeling a sense of shock passing through me at such an unexpected awakening. As my ears slowly returned to normal I looked about, wondering just how far the sound and indeed its accompanying vibrations had travelled. Our nearest neighbours would surely have heard such a thing, and even felt it as I had, but no one could be seen or heard and when my normal hearing seemed to have returned and my heart rate had slowed

9

somewhat, I followed my benefactor back to the barn.

The door lay open, and stepping once more across the threshold and hearing just a low level hum as the machine before me continued to slow, I gazed in awe at the sheer size and imposition of the beast before me. For it was certainly a beast of a machine in my eyes. It resembled in some ways a beam engine, yet even I could see that it was far more than that. The beam itself had come to a full stop by this time, but instead of a standard piston arrangement at one end, I could see a rotating drum of some kind still in its final death throws of motion. To call it a drum seems to understate the sight laid out before me. I'd never seen anything quite like it, and I admit, on some level it frightened me with its sense of raw power. I had the unnerving feeling that this machine was capable of harnessing the unseen forces of nature in a way never before seen.

'Isn't it magnificent, my boy!' The professor gestured proudly at the beast as I continued to stare in wonder. 'I've no doubt that my young student of physics has already determined that this is no ordinary beam engine. It has been quite the undertaking, I must say. I've employed a level of diligence in keeping the true nature and design of the machine known only to me. The parts have been manufactured to my design by separate entities, and those involved in its final construction have only been privy to their own small piece of the puzzle. There've been questions, of course, but to the untrained and uneducated eye, there will be little clue as to its true nature. Come, don't be afraid. Its perfectly safe to approach, although some protection will be required when it's in motion, of course.'

'What is its true nature, Professor?' I asked, walking to the far end of the machine in order to gain a closer perspective. It almost entirely filled the space, and it was as I've explained, a most expansive indoor space indeed. The beam itself when at its highest extent would reach into the roof space itself. The entire thing was built upon a brickwork base that extended almost the entire length of the building.

'Magnetism, my boy. I intend to create the most powerful electro-magnetic field that has even been produced.'

I stopped, looking passed the monolithic beast as I felt a rush of excitement run through me. I would be telling an untruth if I were not to admit to an underlying sense of anxiety too, although some would acquaint this more to hindsight after the fact than an inkling as to what was to come. Nevertheless, I maintain that it was there at the time, even at this early stage in my story.

'To what purpose, Professor?' I asked of him, whilst considering that this may indeed be a purpose in its own right.

'To travel, my boy.' My expression was enough to constitute further elaboration. 'You see, magnetism is one of, if not *the* most powerful forces in nature. The most powerful in Heaven and Earth in fact. What if we were to find a way of harnessing such power. Of controlling it in such a way as to direct its force to attract the very atoms in another place entirely. If we could hold them together, join them if you will, then a link can be created between the two. A link such as this would allow us to simply step from one place to another regardless of how distant they were in geographical terms. My boy, can you imagine? Travelling from London to Paris in the blink of an eye, simply by stepping through a door, or even further, to China or Africa. Why, there could be no limits as to just how far you could travel with a powerful enough magnetic field. To the Moon and back even!'

His words stunned me. It seemed fanciful and delusional to imagine such things, yet I was standing next to a beast that frightened me to the point of thinking it could indeed be capable of just such an unimaginable thing.

'You see, the engine itself is able to create an electro-magnetic force that when a specific level of output is achieved, I'm able to feed this power back into its rotating core and therefore continue to increase its output in a way that far exceeds the capabilities of a standard engine of this kind. It's almost infinite in its capacity, apart from the physical strength of its component parts of course. We'll have to proceed carefully at first.'

'We?'

'Why, yes, William. Now is the time for you to become my assistant in this undertaking. I'll need your help to continue with my work and develop an operational Interspacial Gateway.'

'Interspacial Gateway, Professor?' I'd never heard such a term before, but I quickly supposed that the nature of what the professor was proposing would indeed require its own vocabulary.

'Yes, that seems the most accurate terminology don't you think? A doorway that occupies the space between two disparate points? We'll keep a glossary of terms, of course.'

'Of course.' I supposed that this would be one of my tasks. One that I greatly anticipated as the Professor's assistant.

As I walked the length of the machine I could almost feel the dormant power of the beast (as I was already coming to think of it) lying within. Once alongside my benefactor, he began to explain the design to me in more detail. My studies had served me well as I understood a great deal of the workings he described. The principal of the electromotor element of the design was not in itself new, and the professor was the first to point this out. What was most revolutionary was the way he'd enhanced this element in order to make it self-generating in such a way that it was capable of creating a power output far in excess of anything before it. I felt obligated to ask why he had not published any of his designs for the consideration of his peers in the scientific community. He gave a response that implied he had little in the way of peers in the community, and as much as this may have held some truth, I suspected that even he considered his theory of an Interspacial Gateway somewhat ambitious. For a man such as himself, proof of his theory was far better attained prior to any public reveal. There were those that would waste little time in decrying such a fanciful theory, and indeed those that would like nothing more than to see his reputation plundered.

Henceforth our work begun, and I wasted little time in familiarising myself with the operation of the Beast.

Chapter Three

It became clear within the first few days of my involvement in the professor's life's work that there was still much to do. Although he'd created a most impressive mechanism with which to produce the necessary power output for his invention, the actual gateway itself was still very much a work in progress.

A conduit was required to channel the electro-magnetic power to a gateway. A gateway that was yet to be designed in its entirety. His plans were revealed to me one Friday afternoon as I was helping to reorganise the basement.

'We'll run the conduit from the machine down into the basement. We'll require a secure location for the gateway, so this will be it. Away from any inadvertent discovery, accidental or otherwise.' The professor's concerns over his invention being discovered by his peers did seem to border upon the paranoid at times. A fact that I prudently kept to myself.

'What about the vibrations, Professor?' I looked up from my notes as I recalled the fearful effects of the machine within the house.

14

'Not to worry, young William. I'm introducing a dampening mechanism to reduce the vibrations overall. I did worry for my collection so. We should be safe from any such movements in future.'

His "collection", as he referred to it, was in fact a strange assortment of fossilised remains that he'd assembled over many years. It'd always seemed an odd choice for a man such as he to collect such things. He was concerned with furthering mankind's knowledge. With technological progress the like of which few had dreamed, and yet his fondness for these relics seemed to contradict the man himself. I can recall the only time during my upbringing in his household that I feared the professor would strike me. As an exuberant twelve year old I'd often ran about the house from room to room, careless of the consequences should I lose my footing or trip. The one time I did, I was unfortunate enough to fall against a cabinet that contained a number of these curiosities. Several jars containing fossils fell over and one did indeed break upon the floor. The burst of anger that escaped him when he discovered what had happened quite surprised me. In the end he became calm once more, and I was relieved to find that the item inside had remained intact.

I often stole looks at the varied and somewhat interesting curiosities displayed about the house, becoming almost as fascinated with them as the Professor himself. It was of course with a sense of caution that I did so, wary of causing damage to such precious curiosities. I often wondered whether they provided a visible, tangible link to previous times. A demonstrable reminder of where the world had come from in order to better focus the mind on the possibilities for the future.

'I'm afraid there'll be some physical labour involved, my boy. The conduit will need to be contained underneath the ground. I'll have George bring his boys to help with the labour, but we'll need to complete the work ourselves.'

George was a man that'd proved capable, dependable and above all discreet when it came to undertaking work for the professor. His boys were indeed his sons, and they, like their father, seemed perfectly content to provide their services with little in the way of questions asked. Of course they were paid well for their efforts. A fact that I'm in no doubt contributed greatly to their circumspection.

We had just finished moving the last of his partially complete projects when the front door bell rang from above. We looked at each other in surprise as if neither of us had ever expected such a thing. A cloud of suspicion seemed to immediately fall across my benefactor's features as he eyed the steps leading up to the main house.

'Who can that be?' He asked.

'I'll go, shall I, Professor?' I said, letting go of the rather fragile frame that I was still holding. It was to form part of our project, but as yet I knew not what part it would indeed play.

'Eh? Oh, yes, yes. You do that, my boy. You do that.' I remember noticing how his eyes searched the basement as if assessing the danger that the unseen, and so far unidentified guests, would pose.

I took my leave and headed up the wooden steps to the main house. It was always a moment of relief when stepping from the dingy confines of the basement back out into the world above ground. There were in fact a number of small windows placed on both sides of the basement, but their outlook was only as far as the metal grates above, and the windows themselves were grimy and unkempt. They did at least lend some daylight to the proceedings, yet we quite often required the addition of gaslights when involved in more intricate work.

'Ruthie!' I stood in the doorway like a fool as I set eyes

upon my sweetheart. She smiled, her fair coloured curls cascading about her shoulders, her hands clutching a parasol as it rested upon her shoulder.

Ruthie's smile began to fade as she realised, as did I, that I'd quite forgotten our arrangements. I'd promised to take her for a walk into Regents Park, yet I was hardly dressed for such an occasion.

'Tell me you didn't forget, William. I shall be mad if you did.' She pouted at me as I stood like a fool in the doorway. I'm sure that she would say that it was a failing of mine, but I'd become quite smitten with that pout of hers that so often turned into a coy smile. On this occasion it did not. 'Well, are you going to invite me in or have you quite forgotten your manners too?'

'Oh, yes, I'm sorry, Ruthie. I found myself helping the Professor at an important stage in his work, and I—'

'Who's calling, William?' The Professor called as he exited the basement. He cast his gaze down the hallway and noticeably baulked at the sight of my sweetheart standing there, silhouetted by the sunlight. 'Ah ... erm ...' He fumbled with the basement door for a moment, turning the key and dropping it into his waistcoat.

'It's Ruthie, Professor. We're to be taking a walk in Regents Park this afternoon.' I thought I'd better remind him of her name, lest he fumble with that too.

'Oh, yes, of course.' He nodded vaguely, before turning away and heading to the drawing room, but not before I caught a slight frown upon his brow. 'I'll be taking my afternoon gin.'

The professor quite often indulged in a glass of gin in the afternoons. It was something he quite often used in order to refocus his mind on any given problem at hand.

I am probably remiss in not mentioning my sweetheart Ruthie before now, although I would suppose she has had little relevance in my tale up until this point. Ruthie Doolan and I had been courting for some time, yet I still felt a certain discomfort when presenting her to my benefactor. The main reason for this as I should explain, is that her father was in fact one of the Professor's peers. A member of the British Association for the Advancement of Science, and in Professor Thorebourne's view, his arch nemesis.

It was never entirely clear to me quite why the Professor considered this man in such an unfavourable light. He'd always seemed a gentlemen of honour to myself, and any attempt to question such an opinion had been met with a dismissive wave and a refusal to elaborate further.

The professor had made it clear that Ruthie was not to be given sight of his work, and under no circumstances was she to be allowed near the barn or indeed the basement. I suspect that he imagined she would feel obliged to report upon anything of note to her father, a fellow man of science and learning. Following this latest occasion of a less than polite greeting of my Ruthie, I determined to get to the bottom of such a level of mistrust, if only to lessen my own difficulties.

I showed Ruthie into the dining room, worried that the Professor would be unkind if she were to encroach upon his gin taking. It is not that I believed that a gentleman of my benefactor's nature and standing would deliberately slight a lady in such a way, you understand. It's more that he lacked a certain social ability when it came to masking his true thoughts or feelings.

With a swift change of clothes and some light grooming, I was soon suitably attired to accompany Ruthie on our prearranged walk. I found her examining some of the professor's curiosities as I returned to the dining room, her face screwed up in a look of distaste.

'What are these, William?'

'They're fossils. Remains of animal and plant life from prehistoric times. The Professor collects them.'

'Why?'

'They're quite fascinating, I find. Don't you?' I caught myself defending the Professor's curiosities quite unexpectedly.

'They're rather gruesome, aren't they?'

'I suppose some are, in a way. Shall we go?'

'What is the Professor working on these days? My father says he's hardly been seen at all recently. It almost seems that he's become a hermit.'

Her question surprised me. She'd seldom showed any interest in the Professor's work before, or indeed her own father's. For a moment I found myself regarding my Ruthie with an air of suspicion, quite as if the Professor himself had taken a hold of my thoughts.

'Oh, he's been working on various projects. He gets like that sometimes. He can be quite single-minded at times. Shall we go?'

This time she shrugged, sparing one last disparaging look at the Professor's "gruesome" curiosities before joining me. Our conversations wandered as aimlessly as our feet for the rest of the afternoon, with never a mention of the Professor's work again, yet I couldn't quite discharge such thoughts from my mind of her uncharacteristic interest in the Professor's work. I told myself that it was nothing. That it had simply been an innocent enquiry on her part, nevertheless, the idea was now there. A small seed had been planted, whether as a result of the Professor's ongoing paranoia infesting me, or whether from my own suspicions being triggered by - what? The stilted way in which she had asked? - perhaps. A sense of feigned disinterest picked up upon? - possibly.

We said our usual goodbyes on that day as I left her at her door, but something stayed with me all the same. Something that I disliked in myself. Something that I wish had remained an unfounded notion.

Chapter Four

Two days later and George appeared with his sons. It was a familiar scenario for them. A brief conversation was had as to the work required, and with little involved other than sinking a trench and lining it to protect the conduit, they set about their task with relish. I rather fancy they were being paid considerably more than would normally be the case for such work, but the Professor was comfortable entrusting them and I've no doubt perfectly content with furnishing them with a generous remuneration.

I myself took possession of the conduit as it was delivered to the house by cart, having once again been manufactured to order in the East of the city. It was pulled by two rather unhappy looking ponies that had struggled with their unusual load through the busy streets of London. The trench by this time was two thirds complete and myself and the professor, along with George and his boys laboured to manoeuvre the heavy conduit into place, ready to be connected to the Beast.

I must admit, my excitement was growing already, despite knowing that much work still lay ahead of us. Ruthie was becoming increasingly unhappy with my preoccupation at the house, and her questions had become increasingly more demanding in nature. This did little to assuage my niggling suspicions.

Connecting the rather weighty conduit to the machine proved a surprisingly monumental task. Its thickness prevented it from being easily manoeuvred into place, and it took all five of us to succeed. We made sure that it was securely bolted into place, knowing just how much force could be generated by the Beast. The concerned look upon the Professor's face as he examined the steadfastness of the connections and the placement of the conduit was evidence enough of how undesirable it would be for it to spring loose in the midst of a power transference.

It was finally fed into the basement via one of the small windows, which was entirely taken out for the purpose and filled in around the conduit. Finally we had our connection to the power source, and now we could focus all of our efforts upon the gateway itself.

I had little understanding of how this would work. In comparison it seemed that the machinery to create the electro-magnetic forces needed was far less challenging in its application of scientific and mechanical theories. It is true that I still struggled to comprehend some of the complexities of the machine, but I still felt I had a far firmer grasp upon these than the gateway itself.

'We shall test the theory with a smaller version of the gateway at first,' declared the Professor one day, as I struggled to fit a coupling upon the end of the conduit, now suitably positioned within the basement. 'It will be safer, I fancy, and it will be ready more quickly than the full size version.'

'Indeed,' I agreed. This seemed a most sensible precaution.

'There is little more you can do for now, William.' The

professor peered around the basement thoughtfully. 'You may as well take some time for yourself. I will call upon you once I'm ready for the next stage.'

'If you're sure, Professor?' In truth I was desperate to spend more time with Ruthie, although I would not have said as much. I felt I owed him my time and besides, I was becoming almost as fascinated with his theory as the Professor himself.

'Quite so, William. I know you've had little time to spend with your young lady. I will be quite preoccupied for some time and I can be a little forgetful that you're a young man in the prime of his life. Call on your young lady, if you wish?'

I gave my thanks, watching as he turned back to his work. He retrieved his well-thumbed notebook, its brown leather cover appearing a little threadbare with use. I'd never looked inside at the professor's notes and he'd never shown any inclination to offer. It was his private work. The one place that he scribbled his copious notes whenever a thought struck him or a breakthrough blossomed. It was the Holy Grail of the Interspacial Gateway. An insight into the Professor's mind that as tempting as it might be, I had resisted any move to intrude upon. When the time was right, I considered that I would be made privy to such knowledge by my benefactor.

Chapter Five

I almost rushed from the house in my eagerness to call upon my Ruthie, before realising what an unsightly mess I had become following my labours. It wasn't until I'd cleaned myself up that I began to realise how neglected the household chores had become. The professor employed the services of a woman, Mrs Hill, to help with most things. Which she did with an efficacy that never failed to impress me. However, she also treated us, or in most cases myself, to regular lectures upon the need to provide her with our laundry in a more organised fashion. This was one of those occasions when I realised she had a most valid point. One to which I promised myself that I would heed more diligently in future.

When finally I was able to exit the house more suitably attired, I was wearing a shirt that I decided would remain beneath my coat for fear of its poor appearance proving an embarrassment in front of Ruthie's father, Professor Doolan.

My guilt at rather neglecting Ruthie made me purchase some blooms from a local flower seller as I made my way past Portman Market. I was assailed by the sights and sounds of the busy marketplace and was tempted to dally amongst the stalls selling butcher's meat and poultry for a time, but instead I hastened on to where Ruthie resided close to Regents Park itself. It was a handsome place. Somewhat more refined than my own residence. As always I felt the need to adjust my dress as I entered her street, ensuring I was as well turned out as possible before approaching the steps that led up from the street to their splendid townhouse.

Pulling the bell cord, I waited patiently, observing a local nanny as she took her charges in the direction of the park. I was so absorbed in the comings and goings I was taken quite by surprise when the door opened behind me and the butler spoke.

'Ah, Master Winn, how nice to see you again.'

'And you, Morris. Is Miss Doolan at home?'

'Indeed, Sir. Please come in. I believe she's with her father just now. I'll let them know you're here.'

I stepped inside as Morris held the door. I noted as usual, the stiffness in his leg as he shifted his weight a little awkwardly. Out of politeness I'd never asked about such a thing, but Ruthie had told me that he'd been injured during the Crimean War. In fact, he'd apparently braved the fire of the enemy lines in order to bring back the Professor's injured brother - her uncle, to safety. His actions on that day had failed to save the man's life, but all the same, her father had felt a debt of gratitude to the man that had seen him gain employment with the family despite his own injuries. I thought on many occasions that Morris displayed a certain chariness when it came to anyone outside of the family, as if he were sworn to protect them from enemies, both seen and unseen.

I couldn't help but wonder when these thoughts struck me as to whether either men had known my own father, who'd lost his life in that dreadful conflict, but this too I never asked. For one,

I had no recollection of what the man had looked like, so young was I when he'd been taken away from us, and besides this, it seemed so unlikely that such a coincidence would have manifested itself with so many men involved in the campaign.

The house had a somewhat formal feel to it, which contrasted quite heavily with my own abode. There was nothing in the way of creative whimsies or inventions upon display. It was however, a house meant to impress. To make the visitor feel humbled and maybe a little intimidated by its owners, or possibly this was just my own impression.

The butler disappeared toward where I knew the Professor's study was located at the rear of the house, leaving me to contemplate the small collection of portraits arranged about the hallway. I studied Professor Doolan's portrait, one which he was particularly proud of. It was a recently commissioned painting, showing him holding his recently awarded Mumford Medal from The Royal Society. His name emblazoned upon its surface. A familiar sense of annoyance rose within me, thinking of Professor Thorebourne's distrust of this man and his often hinted at suspicions that the man's discoveries were not entirely of his own making. He'd even accused the man of stealing his own ideas, although this was only said in private and at times when the Professor had imbibed a generous amount of port wine.

'William!' Ruthie called from the far end of the hall. I hadn't heard her approaching and turned in surprise, finding myself forcing a smile to my lips to replace the hard line that'd formed as I considered her father.

'Ruthie, hello. I'm sorry if I've come unannounced, I was rather hoping to spend some time together.'

'Has Professor Thorebourne let you out for the afternoon?'

I detected a note of unhappiness there, and not without

reason I would suppose. I just smiled my best smile and kissed her hand as any young gentleman should in such circumstances.

'Come see my father, William. It's been an absolute age since he's seen you.'

I thought of attempting to sidestep this particular request, but she quickly grasped my hand and began leading me away. It wasn't that I'd experienced anything unseemly at his hands you understand. He'd always treated me with politeness, albeit with an occasional look of disdain - which may have simply been my own mind seeing things that were not really there. He knew of my background of course, and I supposed that knowing of his insights led me to believe that a man of his stature would surely look down upon one with such a background in life.

Ruthie knocked politely upon the door as I looked about, wondering quite where Morris had gotten to. Hearing a voice beckoning from inside, she opened the door and it creaked slightly as we entered.

The study was an impressive sight to behold. Two of the walls were lined with bookcases reaching as far as the ceiling, and they were filled with large and small tomes alike. The professor's desk was positioned in front of the French doors that led out into the garden. The sun streamed in, silhouetting the man amongst the dust motes that floated lazily about the sunbeams. He stood by the window, his arms behind his back, one eyebrow raised in greeting.

'Good afternoon, William,' he said. I couldn't discern whether his tone was amiable or disapproving, such was the manner of the man.

'Good afternoon, Sir,' I replied politely, nodding as I found myself standing in the centre of the room, the ornate desk with its perfectly placed ornamentation between us.

'You've come to call upon my daughter.'

The question seemed rhetorical in nature, yet I felt obliged to offer an answer.

'Yes, Sir. I have some time away from my work and was eager to visit with Ruthie. Perhaps take her for a walk. It's a fine afternoon.'

'Indeed. Wendell appears to be keeping you busy in his employ. How is the Professor? His presence was missed at the last meeting of the Association. I was hoping to hear of his most recent developments.'

Professor Doolan had frequently debunked some of my mentor's more ambitious theories. One other reason for the enmity felt between the two men. It was my turn to raise an eyebrow over his curiosity.

'I'm afraid the Professor was unable to spare the time for travelling, Sir. His work was at a pressing point and—'

'Spare the time? My boy, the British Association for the Advancement of Science is not a social club. It is the preeminent organisation for the promotion of the sciences and is a most prestigious and learned society. It is not something that should be shunned lightly by those involved in the advancement of knowledge.'

I found myself in a most difficult position. I felt rather than saw Ruthie's discomfort at her father's outburst. It would not do, however, for someone like myself to challenge such a gentleman, and certainly not in his own study. 'No, Sir. I'm sure the Professor meant no disrespect by not attending. He follows the Association's progress with great interest.' Which was true enough, despite his frequent disparaging remarks when it came to a number of his peers, particularly the gentleman standing in

28

front of me. 'I'm sure he'll make every effort to attend the next meeting.'

'Quite so, although Belfast is a good deal farther to travel than Bradford, is it not?'

'Father, please. William has come to call upon me, not to be baited about such things,' Ruthie interjected, attracting a rather hard stare from the man before thankfully his expression softened.

'Quite so.' Professor Doolan's shoulders visibly relaxed as his manner altered. 'May I ask the nature of the work that the Professor is undertaking just now that so preoccupies my daughter's young man?'

'Oh, I'm not sure that I would be able to offer a suitable explanation, Sir.' I wasn't entirely certain of how much information I could safely impart upon this man, and so I decided to impart as little as possible.

'Come now, I'm sure that you're able to summarise his intent. The Association would be most interested in following his work, I'm sure.' I was just as sure that he was right, although I suspected Professor Doolan had a uniquely personal interest in such things. 'I hear that he's constructed his very own beam engine. Presumably his work is in relation to furthering such technologies? Although I confess, engineering seems a little ... beneath the man, perhaps?'

The revelation that this man was aware of Professor Thorebourne's engine shook me for a moment, but I quickly reasoned that regardless of any precautions taken at the time, operating an engine of such magnitude would hardly go unnoticed by others for long.

'I believe his work is closely related to the engine, Sir, but I would not presume to offer any further information.' I endeavoured to keep my response light as I felt myself mentally fencing with the man's curious thrusts, no doubt hoping to hoist a valuable morsel of knowledge from me.

The Professor studied me for a while, as if ascertaining how much I really knew of his peer's work. Finally, he grunted somewhat impatiently before dropping into his chair.

'Please see that Wendell gets this, William.' He picked up a sealed letter from his desk and held it out. 'It is an invite to attend the Association's office in Albemarle Street. There is much deliberation underway with regards to electrical standards, and any work being undertaken in the field of electromotivity by the Professor is likely to have a bearing on such a debate. The Association would therefore appreciate his attendance along with a number of other members to further discuss the subject.' I reached out to take it but rather than release the missive into my hand, he pulled it back a little. Our eyes met. 'I would emphasise that the Association would take a dim view if the Professor were unable to, or ... *unwilling* to attend. His reputation as a valued member of the scientific community would not do well, were he to further snub his peers.'

He held it for a moment longer, before finally letting go. I felt myself a little breathless from the encounter. Feeling as though I'd glimpsed something behind those eyes that would do nothing to assuage Professor Thorebourne's view of the man.

'I'll see that he gets it, Professor,' I said, tucking the letter inside my coat as I glanced a little nervously at Ruthie.

'Good. Now, why don't you two take that walk together. It would be a shame to lose what's left of the day's sun.'

I nodded politely before gesturing for Ruthie to leave ahead of me, feeling a little out of sorts.

30

Chapter Six

'Oh come now, William. My father was simply interested in the Professor's work. They *are* both scientists, are they not?'

Ruthie's impatience over my questions was evident as we sat beneath the shade of an ancient looking oak tree in Regent's Park.

'I know, but he seemed to be rather ... forceful, in his questioning. And demanding that the Professor attend this meeting in fear of his reputation being smeared, well—'

'I'm sure he meant nothing untoward, William. You know what scientists are like. They're so preoccupied with their latest work or theories that they forget to avail themselves of the social niceties that people such as ourselves take for granted. You're being silly and more than a little rude about my father.' As was her habit, she gave a sullen pout at my insensitivities.

'Yes, you're right, Ruthie. I'm sorry. I'm being impolite. I apologise profusely.' I took her hand in mine, reminding myself just why I'd been so keen to visit with her. I put all thoughts of her father aside. 'Shall we walk? I thought we may even take a stroll about the zoo, if we have time?'

'Oh yes! I would so like to see the lions again. Such ferocious beasts.'

I took Ruthie to see her lions then. All thoughts of her father and the letter were put out of my mind as we surveyed the animals in the zoo. It was a Monday, I believe, and so the crowds were fewer than on other days. The street lamps were being lit as we returned, and I took my leave without further encounters with Professor Doolan.

-oOo-

'A meeting at their offices! Unheard of, surely. What's the meaning of this?'

I'd found the professor still in the basement upon my return. There was little light to work with but he seemed unable to tear himself away from his efforts.

'That's all that was said to me, Professor. Surely it is innocent enough?'

'Innocent? My dear boy, there is little in Percival's intent that is innocent, I assure you.'

A flash of anger passed across the Professor's countenance, its obvious intensity surprising me still. I was beginning to think that my mentor had quite given leave of any rational beliefs when it came to Ruthie's father.

'He means to have it, you know.'

'What, Professor?'

'Why, the Interspacial Gateway, of course!'

'But, he cannot possibly know of such a thing, surely. His only knowledge is of the beam engine. He seemed to think that your work revolved around this alone. I can think of no manner in which he would know of its true purpose.' His eyes looked wild for a moment as he held me within his questioning gaze.

'Ruthie does not know of anything, besides the engine?' It felt like an accusation more than a question.

'No, Sir. I have told her nothing of anything, not even the engine itself. I know not of where he has procured such knowledge, but it cannot be that such a machine would remain unknown for long, surely?'

The professor's reasoning seemed to return little by little as he considered my words. His benign smile gradually took the place of the firm line of his lips, and his eyes shone back at me as if emerging from a fog of madness.

'Of course, of course. You are quite correct, my boy. Come, let me show you what I have achieved. You will be impressed, I am sure.'

I don't know if I would say I was impressed at this juncture. The Professor presented me with a conductive frame of sorts, about the size of a small painting that was secured upon a stand. He had connected it to the conduit via a junction where the wires snaked their way between the two elements of the machine. As he explained the design, I gathered that the electromagnetic forces produced by The Beast would be directed and focused around the frame itself, and once the output had reached a level suited to creating a magnetic attraction of such force as to be able to link two distant points via the very atoms that made up those points, the power could be unleashed in a directed burst.

33

'How would you determine the point of attraction, Professor?' I asked as soon as the question appeared in my mind. He frowned then, his gaze growing distant for a moment.

'The amount of magnetic force used will have a direct bearing upon the distance over which it can operate. As for the actual location, I admit this may be a matter of experimentation. One thing at a time, dear boy. One thing at a time.'

He soon returned to his work, despite the barely adequate lighting now available to him.

-oOo-

A couple of days passed and I was once more busy with assisting the Professor. Everything seemed ready, yet it was as if the Professor had become reluctant to take the next step. He checked and rechecked his calculations, followed by a step by step examination of all of the components that comprised the gateway. It wasn't until he'd simply run out of things to check upon that he faced me with an almost grim expression.

'It is time, William. We must take the next step in this venture.'

'You seem uncertain, Professor,' I said. 'Is this not the point that you've been working towards?'

'Indeed it is, however, now that we are upon such a moment, I wonder just what manner of natural forces we are about to unleash. This has never been attempted before. It has never been conceived of before. I cannot be so arrogant as to believe there is nothing inherently dangerous in such an undertaking, or that even I have full understanding of those unseen dangers.' He

34

drew a deep breath. 'But, it is time indeed. Let us start the engine and return to the basement swiftly, before the output is sufficiently produced.'

I followed in his steps as we both left the basement. It was a beautiful day outside, and one that I took particular pleasure in at that moment. I told myself that all would be well. That this would not be the last time I felt the breeze upon my neck or the warmth of the sun upon my face, but something inside me would not settle. I was anxious, and I think I had an inkling that our path would not be an easily trodden one to reach such heights of scientific experimentation.

As the boiler was fired up I watched as the steam output grew. It took some time before there was enough to begin moving the beam, and then the wheel began to rotate. The huge dynamo held within the casing was soon being driven at high speed. I moved to where the Professor was monitoring the gauges. He indicated for me to put my ear dampeners on, and we stood side by side as we watched the power increase. The maximum output plateaued and I looked at the Professor.

'I'M SWITCHING ON THE MAGNETIC FEEDBACK LOOP!' he shouted over his shoulder. I could barely hear his words but his meaning was clear enough. As he threw the switch, the power began to rise rapidly once more and I could feel the vibrations through my feet. The dampeners were doing their job, as I fancy it was far less of an effect than I'd felt in the house before, even though we were within feet of The Beast itself. The high-pitched scream grew even through the thick ear dampeners. 'WE SHOULD GO. ALL IS WELL FOR NOW!' The professor pointed to the door and beyond, indicating that we should return to the basement.

I was glad to be out of there. In the presence of such a machine it was as if you could feel its hidden power seething from within. It felt menacing. Almost animalistic in nature. The air itself seemed charged with unseen forces. I guessed The Beast was indeed a most apt name.

We hurried back into the house, and as we headed downward into the basement I had my first thought of how much improved our situation would be if there were a tunnel linking the two locations. A thought for another time, I decided.

A quick check of the instruments revealed that the power was being generated at a frightful speed. The hair on the back of my neck stood up and I felt nauseous.

'Almost there! My, My.' The Professor gazed wide-eyed at the control panel that was bolted to his workbench. His excitement obvious. 'Switching on the Interspatial Linkage - Now!'

He threw a switch, sending the full charge of electro-magnetic output into the gateway. There was a bright flash, blinding me instantly, and then I could feel a surge of power all about me. I thought I would die then. That our time had come and that we'd interfered with the laws of physics in a way that should never have been, and then there was blackness. An abyss that took me away completely.

Chapter Seven

From nothingness, I became aware of feeling. Feeling in my body - my arms and legs mainly. I took a breath and felt life rushing back to me. At first I didn't want to move, but I knew I had to. I had to know what had happened, to both myself and the Professor.

As I opened my eyes I felt a blinding headache strike me and I quickly closed them again, waiting for the worst of the effects to subside. I became aware of a low hum and the telltale vibration of the floor that told me The Beast was still running outside. I forced my eyes wide, and tentatively sat up. Everything seemed to be working and my worst fears of an explosion were unfounded as I realised that the basement itself was apparently unscathed, mostly, at any rate. The Professor had seemingly recovered himself, at least well enough to be assessing the various instruments to ascertain the current situation.'

'Professor?' I asked, feeling a little disorientated.

'Ah, William. You're okay.' He turned briefly, before looking back to his gauges, several of which seemed to have broken.

I looked about, seeing the gateway still in place although a little scorched around the edges.

'What happened?' I asked finally.

'Too much. It was too much power I believe,' he muttered. 'I'll shut down the engine, then we can examine our findings.' He looked a little crestfallen by the whole affair, or maybe he was feeling much like myself.

'Did it work though?'

'Work? It overloaded. I hardly think so, William, do you?'

'What's this?' I bent forward from where I was sat in a most undignified fashion upon the floor. 'Is this a piece of rock? And there ... and there.'

The Professor stopped halfway across the floor and followed my gaze. He looked about, seeing various points of impact about the basement walls.

'Where did it come from?' I asked, still feeling as if in a stupefied state.

There was a pause as the Professor continued to stare. He picked up a small piece of debris by his feet and backtracked to the control panel. I took the time to check that I was indeed in one piece before getting to my feet.

'Magnetite rock,' he said, only deepening my sense of confusion. 'My, My, Magnetite rock. It shouldn't be. It can't be, except ...'

'Except what, Professor?'

'It worked. It damned well worked! Well, I'll be blowed.'
He let out a most uncharacteristic shout of joy before rushing
toward me. I was embraced madly for several seconds before we
broke apart and I continued to stare at him as if watching a
lunatic running about an asylum. 'Don't you see, William? The
gateway connected itself. It connected to a large deposit of
Magnetite, which itself possesses its own magnetic force. There
are no known deposits anywhere near our location for it to have
come from here. It was too much power. It somehow connected
itself to another source - in this case a large natural source, of
magnetic attraction. It pulled through fragments of the rock
before becoming overloaded. Do you know what this means,
William? It works!' I continued to stare, wondering if what he
was saying was true or whether he'd simply lost his senses. 'Of
course, I'll have to develop a way of controlling the power
output. Of avoiding such an uncontrolled burst in future so that
it may produce a more satisfactory connection.' He looked up as
if remembering The Beast. As he rushed to the door he cried,
'To work, William! To work!'

-o0o-

I felt myself increasingly being taken into the Professor's
confidence. As he attempted to work out the flaws in the
gateway's design, I had my opportunity to see first hand his
personal log containing critical design details and theories. Often
he would talk aloud as if speaking to a peer (which I definitely
was not when it came to such advanced scientific knowledge)
and I did my best to contribute where I could. I fear the best I
could do at times was simply to reflect the Professor's own
thoughts, providing in effect a sounding board for his ideas.
Nevertheless, he seemed more than happy with the arrangements
and I was able to learn of some of the most ambitious scientific

theories in existence.

We practically rebuilt the gateway from scratch, and he added a control system that allowed for the output of The Beast to be managed more accurately. It was during this time that I spoke of my rather mundane yet practical idea.

'Professor, I wonder if I might suggest something that could make the operation of the engine more efficient on a physical level.'

'Yes, William, please do,' he said, looking up briefly from a bundle of wiring that he was attempting to tidy away.

'I wonder if it might be helpful to construct a tunnel between the barn and the basement, in order to better communicate between the two and aid our passage from one to another?' The professor looked up again, appearing surprised by my suggestion. 'Not to worry, I just—'

'My dear boy, that is an excellent suggestion, and one which I'm mystified as to why this never occurred to me. In fact, we could extend the engine controls through the tunnel and integrate them into a single control panel. Yes, indeed, an excellent suggestion, William. Please, feel free to contact George and his boys as soon as you can. My, My, why didn't I think of such a thing?'

And so, George and his sons were soon back to carry out their next labouring task.

'I jus' wish the Professor 'ad mentioned it afore. It woulda made sense to do it before laying the conduit,' George commented as we assessed the work in question whilst walking between the barn and the house, holding his cap and scratching his head with one hand as his two sons watched from afar.

'I'm sorry, George,' I offered. 'We didn't think of it before but it seems so obvious now.'

He nodded sagely, saying, 'Well, I've always got time for the Professor. You just let me know if you need anything else. I'll 'ave me boys make a start in the morning, once we've worked it all out.' And so the next phase of construction commenced.

There could be no more tests of the machine whilst the tunnel was dug out and a series of additional control rods and connectors were laid, although the Professor seemed fully engaged in recalculating and adjusting the design so as not to seem too impatient. Some additional hands were brought in to help, although we made sure to keep the barn, and especially the basement, off-limits to any prying eyes.

As the time passed I realised the date of Professor Doolan's invite was nearing and decided to mention this, in case the Professor had quite forgotten as he was prone to do over such trivialities, as he would see them. I was also reminded several times by my Ruthie, as if she herself had some stake in his attendance which I mistakenly pointed out one afternoon. It led to a rather unseemly altercation, after which I was treated to her most sullen of pouts for the following two days.

The work progressed at a surprisingly rapid rate, and the communication tunnel was soon covered over. There were only two days left before the Professor's summons to the offices of the Association and he seemed increasingly anxious to complete another test of the gateway.

'We'll test the new control system this morning, William,' he said as we were taking breakfast in the dining room. 'We need to confirm that the engine can be controlled correctly from the new station. Then, we shall be ready for the second full test. I'm confident that the power output can be regulated to a good degree of accuracy this time. We should see no repeat of the previous results.'

'Professor, I was wondering if you would like my attendance at the Association's office on Thursday morning?'

'What's that?' He looked up from his eggs, his thoughts clearly with the gateway's upcoming test. 'Association?'

'Yes, Professor. If you recall, Professor Doolan sent you an invite to meet with a number of your peers.' His expression remained quizzical. 'Regarding the debate upon electrical standards, I believe.'

'Electrical standards?' Understanding grew behind his expression and his face turned into a grimace of sorts. 'Indeed, I do recall. Thursday, you say? I suppose I can spare the time, although I must confess, the entire enterprise would seem an unnecessary distraction from my work.'

I waited in silence before asking once more, 'Should I attend too, Professor?'

'Mmm? Oh, no, no, that won't be necessary, my boy. There'll be little of interest to you I would imagine, and the boiler may need some attendance on your part. The engine will need to be fully operational as I intend to continue testing.' The Professor was soon back to his distracted self as we finished our breakfast.

Chapter Eight

We ran through a series of checks in the barn that morning before firing up the boiler and retreating to the basement through the barely lit and newly constructed communications tunnel. We had to shuffle along with our heads bowed and our shoulders hunched, so low was the ceiling, but it still offered a more direct and considerably more discreet passage between the two locations.

Another series of checks followed as we confirmed that the steam pressure was now building and that The Beast was able to commence its operation.

'Here goes, my boy!' Cried the Professor like an excited child as he pulled the lever that opened the valves via a series of control rods.

There was a pause of anticipation before the tell-tale vibration began to transmit through the floor and we could see the power output rising. The sound from the engine was louder than before, communicated directly through the tunnel as it now was. We both donned our ear dampeners as we observed the outputs rising steadily.

'Ready to engage the Magnetic Feedback Loop.' He called, before flicking the switch.

The power rose rapidly once more and the sound increased in its intensity. The vibrations grew more pronounced but no more than on the previous attempt. The smile on the Professor's face told me that all was well. I was glad not to be standing so close to The Beast itself this time, as the raw power of the machine could not be felt so intensely, although it was still there all the same. It's presence had an almost ethereal feel.

'Put these on.' The professor plucked a pair of thick goggles from the bench and handed them to me. I looked at him questioningly. 'The light from the gateway was most intense last time. These will help,' he explained.

I took them from him, seeing that the glass was quite dark in colour. The professor put his on before donning his top hat. I'm not certain why. It was almost out of a sense of ceremony I suppose, as we once more tested the very boundaries of natures forces.

The surroundings grew dim as I followed suit. The gauges were showing that the output had now reached the threshold required for the Gateway's operation. I watched as the Professor adjusted the control dial that had been installed since that first attempt. It required two hands to move it sufficiently as he placed it at the lowest setting.

'This is it, my boy.'

We exchanged anxious looks tinged with barely contained excitement as his hand lingered upon the final switch. I nodded once, acknowledging what was to come, and he threw the switch without hesitation.

I thought I sensed a rush of power flow through the

basement as a bright light flashed outwards. Despite the goggles I found myself turning away in that instant, partly because of the intensity of that flash, and partly because I expected another explosive event. When nothing happened I opened my eyes. At first I just stared at my own shadow where it hadn't been before, its clear lines a testament to the brightness that was now being thrown across the room, but then I noticed a second shadow to one side, less clear, but seeming to indicate more than one light source.

I turned about, seeing the gateway itself, a steady light shining outward as if looking through a window into bright sunlight. There was no explosive event. No rocks were strewn about the basement this time, but to my utter astonishment there was now a second light to my side. There was no frame around the outside. It was as if it floated in mid-air. An apparition that defied explanation, except, we both knew what this had to be.

Another exchange of looks, and then as if testing the very floor that we were stood upon, both the Professor and myself began to creep forward. I looked from one light source to the other, before daring to step behind the second one. Its light was not quite so intense, and as I looked at it from behind all I could see was a kind of blurred outline, as if the air itself were out of focus.

'Professor?' I asked, not quite able to ask the question.

'Yes, my boy. What you are seeing ... what we are both *observing*, is both ends of an Interspacial Gateway. Two points in space drawn together by the magnetic forces of the universe. The very atoms themselves joined with one another as a result of a highly focused burst of electromagnetic force.'

'Professor, you did it. You actually did it!'

'Of course my boy. It's simply a matter of physics, you see.'

'But, how do we know if it's really a gateway. I mean—'

'Can an object or indeed a person pass through such a gateway?'

'Yes.'

'That is our next stage, William. We will test the Gateway. First, we shall pass through an inanimate object. It is too soon to risk life or limb, don't you think?'

I nodded, looking around the basement as I was overcome with the need to pass something through the Gateway. To see for myself whether this was real or simply a light trick, however unintended, as I truly believed the Professor thought that he'd achieved what most would consider the impossible.

A spanner was the first thing that came to hand, and I held it up in the air, asking for the Professor's approval. He raised an eyebrow and a finger as if to question me, before smiling and nodding. As I approached the frame, with the Gateway glowing intensely from within, I wondered briefly whether this was a good idea. For a moment I considered the spanner, hoping it was perfectly expendable and not particularly crucial to the maintenance of the machine, before turning my head and throwing it through. I'm not certain quite what I expected to happen; an explosion of light perhaps, for the spanner to rebound and fly back at me, or for the entire basement to be engulfed in a conflagration of unknown proportions - which in turn questions my reasoning in so doing, but none of these happened. The only result was that a clatter from across the basement could be heard as the spanner dropped to the floor.

We both turned and stared, neither of us apparently expecting to see it reappear as it did so. Our faces were lit with a mirrored joy at having so easily verified the existence of the Professor's Gateway. Two points in space had indeed been

46

joined, and an object had managed to travel through this Gateway from one side of the basement to the other.

The Professor threw his arms in the air and shouted. I found myself laughing quite uncontrollably at the wonder of such a thing, as I hurriedly crossed the space to retrieve our inanimate test subject. It was as I plucked the heavy metal implement from the floor that I realised all had not gone quite to plan. The spanner no longer resembled a spanner, in fact. There seemed little doubt that it was the same object that I'd thrown through the Gateway, given the metallic nature and weight of the thing, but it was now a very different looking object to before.

I looked at the Professor, my joy crumbling inside of me as I tried to understand what had happened. He soon took note of my change in mood and stalked anxiously toward me, suspecting I feel that all was not well.

'What is it, my boy? Show me,' he asked, coming to stand next to me as I held out the resulting mess of metal. 'Oh my!' He took it from my hand, holding it up as he examined it more closely. 'Oh my!' He repeated. 'This won't do. No, this won't do at all.'

I watched him return to the control panel, and a moment later he had thrown the switches to cut the power to the Gateway and disengaged the steam valves from the engine. Nothing was said for some time as he turned the metal object over and over in his hands. Sensing the absence of engine noise and vibrations, and seeing that the light had disappeared from the gateway, I pulled off my goggles and ear dampeners.

'What happened, Professor?' I asked, unable to stop myself although I knew now was probably too soon to gain any insights.

'Hmm? Happened? Well, I would say that the Gateway is ...

unstable, or ... or that the magnetic field is too powerful to allow an object to pass through intact.'

He continued to study what was left of the spanner as I gazed unhappily down the tunnel. 'I'll check the boiler and make sure that the engine is fully shut down, Professor,' I muttered, unwilling to draw him from his contemplation.

I felt a strange mixture of elation and frustration that day. We'd done it, or rather, the Professor had done it. He'd created an Interspacial Gateway that had allowed for an object to pass between two disparate locations instantaneously, although not in a stable manner. I shuddered at the thought of what such a thing could do to a person and was glad that I hadn't been tempted to put my arm inside of the frame, but in the back of my mind I knew that just such a thought had occurred to me, if only for a brief moment. I shuddered once more.

-o0o-

The mood of the Professor was hard to discern for the rest of the day. He barely left the basement, until eventually he was forced to retire to the main house given the lack of light. Even so, he continued to peruse his notes, frantically scribbling as he hypothesised as to the failings of the Gateway. I recognised that it was best to leave him to his thoughts, and other than ensuring that he had what food and drink he required, or was willing to accept, I made my excuses and took it upon myself to visit Ruthie.

Chapter Nine

The afternoon of the Science Association meeting, Professor Thorbourne had me gathering together his notes upon the subject of electrical measurements and his own preferred standards. He had little interest in hearing what his peers had to say on the subject at this time, but nevertheless, he determined that if he was to be a participant in such matters then he would at least offer some valuable contributions to the discussions.

'I don't doubt that there is good reason to establish such standards, my boy,' he explained to me as he donned his coat and hat, with me holding his case that was now full to bursting with anything of relevance that could be found. 'But why this could not wait until the next full meeting of the Association, I do not know. I suppose we may present a proposal paper to the Association for further discussion. It's just, I have so much to do, don't you think? Well, I suppose I can spare one afternoon for such distractions. Don't let me keep you, young William, you have much to do yourself.'

I handed his case over and watched him step out of the door. He intended to walk to Albemarle Street, saying that the air will at least help him postulate on the next steps in his testing.

He'd left me with a number of tasks, the least favourable of which was greasing a number of engine components. I will admit to the temptation of putting such a task off for another day, or even to my shame, of claiming that I'd completed the greasing when I had not, but my conscience prevailed and in a bid to put it out of my mind, I headed to the barn with the intention of completing the work in the quickest time possible.

As always I found myself staring up at The Beast with a sense of awe, gazing across the enclosed machine with its hidden dynamo within. It was perfectly quiet apart from a number of drips falling from the roof following the earlier rain shower, which echoed through the space as The Beast sat idly on its platform, as if in a deep slumber.

I almost crept across the space as I retrieved the bucket of grease and set about what I considered a rather unsavoury task.

I suppose I'd been about my work for at least half an hour when I heard something below. I was hanging in a most awkward position, lubricating the linkages high above the engine itself when a sound other than the incessant dripping reached my ears. At first I thought it was my imagination, but as a second noise echoed through the space I stopped what I was doing and lay still, trying to discern from whence it had come. Then, a voice. Low and indistinct, but certainly a voice. A male voice.

If it had been the voice of a woman I would have assumed that it was Mrs Hill, or even Ruthie, come to pay me an unexpected visit.

The scuff of a foot drew my attention and I craned my neck to look beyond the oversized lever that spanned the top of the machine between the linkage to the crank and the piston arm. I almost lost my handhold and had visions of falling onto the sloping dynamo housing before sliding off the edge, coming to an ignominious and painful end on the solid floor below. I took a breath, steadying my breathing before deciding it would be safer to make my way down to ground level.

I heard nothing else as I clambered down the ladder, but it may be that I was so focused on getting down in one piece that I missed any further disturbances. Once down, I edged along the side of the machine, out of sight of the main space. I don't know why I was being so careful, as I had no reason to believe that anything untoward was afoot. Even so, a tingling at the nape of my neck kept me from calling out to the unexplained visitors.

Just as I began to think that it was my imagination, or that perhaps an animal of some kind had ventured through the open door, I heard a clang of something hitting metal closely followed by a loud exclamation. It was definitely a man's voice.

Feeling that I should make more of a show of myself and challenge whomever this uninvited person was, I gathered my nerves together, straightened my back and marched out from behind the engine. At first I didn't see anyone, but then, appearing from the other side of the dynamo housing, I saw a man walking in a stoop, rubbing his knee.

'Can I help you, Sir?' I asked in a loud voice. Maybe a little too loud, I thought.

The man looked up in surprise, his eyes widening beneath his cap as he realised there was someone else present. Looks were exchanged and I could sense the man sizing me up. I thought for a moment he was some ruffian, intent on robbery, but as I looked I began to see the smart clothing of a man not accustomed to the life of a common thief.

'I say, who are you and what is your business?' I asked, sounding somewhat braver than I felt.

As I stepped closer he seemed to consider his next actions before turning about and running to the door. The sudden movement caught me off-guard and I was slow to follow. As I reached the rear of the property he climbed over the fence and continued to run. I pursued him at a distance, knowing I would likely not catch him and unsure of whether he would be armed.

The man managed to make it back to the street via a circuitous route that left me breathing hard by the time I saw him clamber into an awaiting carriage. It was difficult to see inside, but for a moment I was sure I recognised the man beckoning the driver on as he pulled his accomplice inside, a look of annoyance upon his face.

I returned to the house feeling somewhat ruffled by what had happened. I couldn't be sure of the intruder's motives, but I was certain that the Professor would share my suspicions. Suspicions that left me in a state of disquiet for the rest of the afternoon.

-oOo-

'And you are quite sure, my boy, that you recognised the man? You don't think you were mistaken?' Asked the Professor, squeezing my arm anxiously as he looked me in the eye.

The Professor had returned from the Association's office some two hours after my unsavoury encounter, and I'd had plenty of time to think back upon the events. I'd searched the house, and especially the basement, for any signs of robbery and had found none, leading me to the conclusion that I'd discovered the intruder before he could achieve his ends. The Professor was in a high state of vexation at the news, which I felt obliged to pass on as soon as he'd returned.

'I'm almost certain, Professor,' I said, thinking back to the brief moment that the second man had been visible to me. 'I mean, I suppose it's possible it was another, someone with more than a passing resemblance, but I was sure at the time it was indeed Morris.'

'Why would Professor Doolan's man be behind such a thing? Unless ...' I could see the Professor's mind whirring with possibilities. '... Unless, they were after my research, or to uncover what I'm working upon. Yes, that's it, that must be it. Professor Doolan's invitation was a deception ... a ruse. That would explain it. He wanted me out of the house, so that his man could rifle my notes and uncover my newest project!'

'But what about me, Professor? Why did they think the house was empty?'

'They probably expected you to accompany me to the office. I detected a note of disappointment at your absence. The Professor asked me as to your whereabouts. It would have been too late to get word to his man by then who was undoubtedly watching the house, or at least the man's accomplice would have been. He made the mistake of thinking it was only me that was to leave.' He let go of my arm, looking about the hallway as if on the verge of panic before his expression changed and he clenched his jaw with a determined look. 'We'll have to proceed at a more rapid pace. Do you think they saw anything, William? Did they get to the basement?'

'I ... I don't think so, Professor. I believe the man's main target was the barn. If Professor Doolan believes your work to be based around the engine, then that's where they would look first, isn't it?'

'Quite right, my boy, quite right indeed. The question that now vexes me is whether to challenge Professor Doolan upon this most insidious development. We have no proof, of course, and it would do little to advance my cause within the Association if I were to cast unfounded aspersions upon a fellow member. No, we must take precautions, but our main objective must be to continue my work. To prove my theories and produce a paper in order to evidence my work before Professor Doolan can uncover the true nature of my experiments. Come, William, we have no time to lose.'

The Professor returned to his work with renewed purpose, his efforts tinged with an urgency that demonstrated just how concerned he was that his rival was set upon stealing his very ideas from beneath him. I'd never seen the Professor like this before. He cleared the dining table of any of its normal paraphernalia and spread his notes and drawings about with abandon. He was like a man possessed, scribbling away as he mumbled furiously under his breath. I tried to be of service as much as possible, but was soon set back upon my tasks of maintaining and preparing the engine for the next test, which I determined to fulfil as best I could, it being an important part of my duties as the Professor's assistant.

Chapter Ten

Over the next few days the Professor made several adjustments to the machine, followed swiftly by the firing up of The Beast before his changes were put to the test. We lost several more tools to the ravages of the Interspacial Gateway before it was decided that we'd only use objects that were of no practical use from then on. His incessant mutterings were becoming a source of worry, and I was beginning to think that he may be losing his mind. It took another week before any breakthrough was made. A week that saw my relationship with Ruthie become ever more distant, not least because of my belief that her father was in fact behind a plot to possess the Professor's theories for himself.

It was as I was bringing the Professor his afternoon Gin, a habit that he showed no signs of foregoing regardless of what he was doing at the time, that he turned to me with a distant look in his eyes, as if seeing me, but not entirely.

'The field is too unstable,' he said. I thought for a moment he was waiting for a reply, but then he continued in a quiet yet steady voice. 'The atoms are being joined in an almost random pattern, but not entirely. It's as though a scattering effect is being produced through the gateway, or before the magnetic field has even created the gateway. I need ... I need to stabilise the atomic pattern in such a way as to stop them from being scattered. To introduce a uniform structure to the way the atoms are being joined. That's it. That's the problem.' His brow furrowed deeply as I continued to act as his focal point, despite my inability to offer any further insights. 'But how ... how do I produce a more uniform attraction between atoms so as to produce a stable gateway?' He stared without seeing until I became quite unsettled by it all.

'Your Gin, Professor,' I offered somewhat lamely.

He took it without a word, swigging back a mouthful before staring down at the glass in his hand.

'A stable gateway,' he pondered aloud. 'A structure. That's it, my boy! That is indeed it! I will engineer a second electromagnetic framework in such a way as to create a stable atomic attraction between the two, before the Gateway is fully opened beyond. I will create a structured magnetic field that will then be projected in a stabilised state to the target point in space.' He looked up at me as if having seen the answer in the glass. 'What do you think, William. Do you concur?'

'I ... Um ... It sounds perfectly feasible, Professor,' I said, with little conviction in my own words.

'I'll start at once. In fact, I'll proceed to the full sized electromagnetic framework. There's little time to be wasted and I'll not spend a moment more on caution. Now is the time to take a leap, my boy, and leap I shall!'

His renewed vigour was a joy to behold, and also a little scary, if I'm perfectly honest.

Over the next few days The Beast was in regular operation. We'd even received several enquiries from our closest neighbours as to whether we were now operating a factory of sorts in our barn. Their concerns didn't appear to be fully satisfied by the Professor's assurances that this was but a temporary period of research and development, but they left us alone for the most part.

There was soon a duplicate framework in place which worked in tandem with the first, and several tests later the Professor was happy that nothing too untoward was affecting the objects being flung through the glowing portal, although the first time he attempted a living test subject, in this case one of his favourite Aspidistras, it unfortunately reappeared looking somewhat shredded about the edges. This seemed to dampen his mood for a while as he worried just what effect this would have on a human subject.

It was as I was preparing myself to meet with Ruthie, as I was dressing in my room in fact, that I learnt of the Professor's decision to increase the power to the Gateway by a marginal amount in a bid to overcome what he'd called low interspatial velocity effects.

'It is my increasing belief, William,' he explained that morning as if lecturing to a theatre full of physics students, 'that travelling through an Interspacial Gateway at too slow a speed, can in fact expose the subject to the tremendous forces involved within the magnetic field to the point of which they are literally being pulled apart. That the best way of avoiding such damaging consequences is to actually increase the power of the electromagnetic fields in order to also increase the interspacial velocity between the two points.'

I was in the process of pulling on my trousers, already aware of The Beast running in the barn in order to facilitate yet more tests, that I noticed my shadow appear upon the floor in front of me. I was in fact facing the window at the time, even so, it took a few moments for me to realise quite why this phenomena had gripped my thoughts so. The shadow was in sharp relief, and I became aware of a light source behind me, when quite unexpectedly I felt someone touch my shoulder. I span around so quickly that I quite lost my balance and landed in a most undignified heap upon the floor. As I looked up with surprise, my heart pounding in my chest, I saw a disembodied hand floating in mid-air, with a bright light behind it in the shape of a door. I gasped, trying to force some intelligible words from my mouth, but the shocking sight of a hand moving about in thin air without a body attached had entirely taken my breath away. Eventually I was able to draw a deep breath as I understood what was happening.

'Professor?' I asked of the hand, as if expecting it to form a mouth of its own and speak. 'Is that you?' I realised almost as soon as I'd asked, that it could hardly be anyone else, and that my question would sound somewhat witless.

'William, was that you, my boy?'

'Y-Yes, Professor. Your hand touched me.'

'Excellent! I wasn't sure how far the increase in power would take me.' It was a very surreal conversation to be having with a disembodied hand. 'You can hear me too? Most interesting. Sound waves are able to pass through the Gateway too. Most interesting indeed.'

A few seconds later the hand withdrew itself as the Gateway disappeared, leaving me feeling somewhat disquieted.

Just as soon as I was able to finish dressing I rushed down to the basement. This had certainly been a breakthrough in the Gateway's construction, and one I needed to be party to.

The professor was beaming delightedly as I appeared on the

stairs and he was quick to explain what'd happened. He'd tried several more plants as he increased the power levels slowly but surely. He'd apparently found one in the drawing room and another in the hallway where they'd dropped to the floor on the other side. The last two were quite intact, although he'd tweaked the power levels a little just to be sure before he threw caution to the wind and thrust his own hand through on the last attempt.

I told him he was lucky he still had his hand, but he waved off such concerns in the pursuit of science. I wish now I'd pressed my point a little further, but his increasing paranoia with regard to Professor Doolan's intentions was now driving him on at an almost reckless rate. A recklessness that would soon cost innocent lives, I'm ashamed to say.

Chapter Eleven

The day came when the Professor made the decision to pass through the Gateway himself. I offered up an argument to the contrary, and even offered up myself in his place.

'But Professor, what if it's not safe? You could be killed. And what of your research were such a tragedy to unfold?'

'My dear William,' he looked upon me that day in the basement with a mixture of patience and pity, I thought. 'We must have the courage of our own convictions at times like this. It is now or never. If I delay until I have removed all risk then I will simply be handing over such a discovery to others. Others that may even now be working against me, or at the very least, in competition with me. This is my discovery, William. I've worked for too long to let it slip from my grasp through a lack of courage. We will test it now, but to be on the safe side, we shall increase the power to ensure a safe interspacial velocity.'

'Where will we open the Gateway to, Professor.'

'Well, that is the problem, is it not? We still have little control over where the Gateway will link to. With this in mind we'll need to exercise some caution, at least.'

We donned our ear dampeners and goggles, the Professor placing his hat upon his head and straightening his coat as if about to attend church. I scurried along the tunnel to check that all was well as The Beast was firing up, and to ensure that the doors were now secure in case of any uninvited guests making an appearance. Checks that we'd begun to undertake as a direct result of the intruder.

As I arrived back in the basement, rising to my full height and stretching my back with relief, we exchanged nods and the Professor threw the switch. The air hummed as The Beast began to generate its enormous power. The dial was set a little higher than before, but still on a relatively low setting. As the gauges indicated that the power levels had plateaued, the Professor switched on the feedback loop and the levels began to rise once more.

'We cannot be sure of what will await us on the other side, so we'll exercise caution before stepping through and test for any unseen resistance.'

He lifted up a long pole to demonstrate his intention to test the Gateway's exit by actually poking a pole through to the other side. I couldn't help but look at him with raised eyebrows. It seemed a particularly crude method, but one I supposed would provide a clear enough result.

The Professor was grinning like a maniac as he activated the electromagnetic frames and the sudden flash of brightness still took me by surprise as I watched the Gateway spring into life. We looked at each other. I felt a tension inside of me that I knew was the result of my burgeoning fears for the Professor's safety, but I could do nothing to dissuade him from the most ambitious test yet.

He stepped forward, dropping the long pole down to the horizontal like a knight readying his lance. With one last nod of his head, he focused his attention on the glowing portal and took a determined step forwards. The end of the pole passed into the Gateway without incident. He took another step, and another. As the pole steadily disappeared within the Gateway, it was apparent that no resistance could be found on the other side. He stood there, within reach of the portal itself as he held onto the pole, before slowly withdrawing. The length of wood emerged unscathed in its entirety, and it seemed there was nothing else to do but witness the first ever journey through an Interspacial Gateway by my mentor.

I clasped my hands in front of me, my legs feeling a little unsteady as he placed the pole gently upon the ground and stepped up to the light. He lifted his ear dampeners away from his head and leaned closer, listening. I found myself trying to listen too, before realising I was still wearing my own dampeners and removing them. The noise from The Beast was bearable now, and I moved closer to hear whatever the Professor was listening to, if anything at all.

I stopped by his shoulder and my mouth dropped open. The sounds of people talking, or more accurately shouting, came through the Gateway. It seemed that the portal had caused a stir somewhere else in the world, but quite where I couldn't know. I could only imagine the shock of those people as they saw a door shaped light appear from nowhere, closely followed by a long pole being thrust toward them. It must have made quite a sight indeed.

'Professor, there're people on the other side,' I hissed in my excitement, knowing that he was fully aware of this fact, but unable to stop myself from stating the already known.

Just then the Gateway seemed to flutter, somehow. The light

rippled in a way that I'd not seen before. I looked to the Professor and it was clear that he'd seen the same thing as I.

'What was that?' I asked, watching as another ripple seemed to run through the light's surface.

The Professor turned to the control panel, before saying, 'I'm not certain, William. It may be nothing but I am minded to shut down the Gateway and carry out some checks before testing it further. I have not run it at such a power level until now, apart from that very first attempt.'

He stepped away from the Gateway and began examining the gauges. I turned back to the light in time to see another ripple appear and disappear. It was an interesting phenomena to watch. I continued to stare as I became aware of the voices growing louder from beyond the light. I glanced at the Professor as he bent to take a closer look at his instruments, before turning back to the Gateway. Another ripple appeared, larger this time, more pronounced, and then - a finger. At first I wasn't sure what I was seeing as it disappeared back into the light, but then it reappeared closely followed by the rest of the hand. Someone was at the other side of the Gateway, probing its unseen depths.

'Prof-Professor?' I gasped as a wrist appeared and the hand seemed to wave at me, but I knew its owner could not possibly see me or anything else behind the glowing doorway. Still, I experienced the faint temptation to wave back as I continued to watch. 'PROFESSOR!' I called again, more insistently. The hand disappeared once more, just as the Professor turned around in response.

'What is it, William?'

'The Gateway, Professor. Look!'

He fixed his gaze upon the light just in time to see a number of pronounced ripples emanating from where the hand had appeared at their epicentre. He continued to stare, one eyebrow raised with intense curiosity.

'A disturbance in the field?' He asked no one in particular as he looked back to his instrumentation. 'We must shut down momentarily. Check that all is well before we proceed.'

'No, Professor, there's someone—'

I'm not sure that he heard me at this point as my words died upon my lips. Another disturbance appeared, higher than the first, closely followed by another, then another. Before I could comprehend what was happening, three heads emerged through the doorway. Three men with their eyes tightly closed against the brightness. I felt my legs grow weak as I watched all three tentatively opening their eyes, and realising that they had in fact gained the other side of the mysterious doorway of light, they each looked up, inane grins spread across their faces as they tried to process what they were now seeing.

One was clearly older than the other two. His sparse grey hair lank and greasy looking. A scar ran down one cheek, causing his left eye to droop. His pale blue eyes blinked several times before he began to laugh. It was the laugh of a drunken man. Of one who's senses had been dulled, and who's comprehension was slow to develop. The second one was younger, his long dark hair hiding his features apart from a rather pronounced nose. His mouth slowly opened as he peered about the basement in which he now found himself, or at least a part of him. The third had red hair and a beard. He turned his head first one way then the other, giggling stupidly as he tried to understand what he was now looking at.

I guess they'd only appeared for a couple of seconds at the most, but as I heard the Professor switching the power off to the Gateway, time seemed to slow. I saw everything as if time itself

64

had decided to let me witness the horror that was about to befall us in all of its glorious and sickening detail.

The shout that escaped me was one of desperation. It was already too late, I knew. As the power was shut down, the Gateway flickered. I could only continue to stare at the men that had so foolishly, yet understandably, tried to look beyond that shining portal of light. I saw to my utter dismay that momentary look of confusion in their faces as the very atoms in their bodies were separated as the Gateway lost its connection through space. They seemed to hang there even as the light dimmed around them and the basement behind came into view through the framework, and then they fell. Three disembodied heads with their eyes full of uncomprehending wonder dropping like stones onto the hard floor below. The thud of their skulls impacting the basement floor was sickening to the core. My body felt weak, my stomach churned. The head nearest to me, the older man with grey hair, landed heavily, and as if to add the cruelest of insults to injury, it bounced before coming to rest facing me. I saw his eyes swivel in his head to look up questioningly and our eyes locked for one brief moment that I will never forget for the rest of my days. I saw the life fade from his eyes. The light go out as his lips twitched and his question went unasked. I cannot even imagine what thoughts passed through his mind at the point he found himself being wrenched from his body, his head falling in such an ignominious fashion.

I fell to my knees then, just as the Professor had turned to see the three disembodied heads land at our feet. The Beast was winding down now, its sound diminishing to leave a heavy silence in the basement.

'Oh my!' The Professor exclaimed. I glanced up at him, seeing his wide-eyed expression as he absorbed what had just happened. 'Oh my,' he said again, looking from one head to another as my body shook from head to toe.

'Wh-What have we done?' I asked, after some time had passed with neither of us moving.

'This is most ... unfortunate,' said the Professor, taking off his hat and goggles in a gesture of respect. 'Most unfortunate indeed.'

Chapter Twelve

It was some time before I felt enough strength returning to my legs to be able to stand. The grey haired man continued to stare at me lifelessly, and I had to do something, anything to break that moment. There were several old sacks piled in one corner, behind the Gateway, and I walked somewhat unsteadily over to them, trying not to look at the heads as I passed them. I threw a sack over each one, covering them up and dispelling the paralysis that had seized the Professor.

As a sombre quietude settled across the basement, I walked back to the Professor's side, unwilling to speak too loudly out of respect for the dead men's heads.

'What should we do, Professor?' I asked. 'Those men are ... dead now, because of us.'

'Yes, William, they are. I'm afraid there is little to be done for them now.'

'But what of their families? There will be a scandal. People will want to know how this happened. Who was responsible.'

'Scandal?' The Professor turned to me, placing his hand upon my arm, his face white and pallid looking. 'William, we do not even know whence these men came from. Their ... bodies, could be anywhere in the city, the country, the world even. We have no way of identifying them ourselves, and unless a story appears in the papers regarding these three unfortunate fellows, we may never know who they were or where they came from.'

'But ... we have to do something, Professor, surely?' I pleaded, not really knowing what I thought should happen.

'Yes, yes you're right, William. Quite right, indeed.' The Professor took a step closer to the sacks that now hid the macabre results of his experiment. 'They deserve to be buried. Buried properly and with respect, even though we may not be able to provide them with headstones to mark their graves. In the potting shed you'll have seen my coffin.'

The Professor now referred to what I had always found to be a rather disturbing possession of his. His late brother, a man that had found himself in sole charge of a funeral parlour following his father-in-law's death had, prior to his own demise, decided to furnish his brother with a particularly well made example of his work. The rather obscure and in my opinion, morbid gift, was the result of the Professor idly admiring the object on one of his rare visits to his brother's emporium some twelve years previously. In my mind I now envisioned its resting place for the past ten years at least, where it'd gathered dust and cobwebs standing up in the corner of a seldom used shed.

'Have it laid out upon the bench and we can place the ... remains inside, pending a suitable burial opportunity. I have little interest in the coffin myself, although my brother believed me to be quite taken with it for some reason.'

The prospect of handling the three unfortunate men's heads was an unsettling one to say the least, but I knew that we could

68

not call upon another to aid in such a task. This had to be dealt with by ourselves alone. I shuddered to think of what might happen were someone to discover three heads in the basement. Even if the Professor were to reveal his invention and the unfortunate manner of the men's deaths, it was doubtful that his story would be believed. I imagined us both finding ourselves on trial for murder, the consequences of which seemed too bleak to think upon.

With a sinking feeling inside of me, I approached the three sacks, trying hard not to think of what lay underneath. I crouched next to the first, and with several deep breaths behind me and a monumental effort to think of anything other than the act of which I was now engaged upon, I lifted the sack. The head shifted slightly as I did so, almost bringing a scream of fright from my lips. For a moment I was captivated by the macabre sight afore me. There was surprisingly little blood to be seen, although I dread to think of just how much may have been present alongside the decapitated body in its distant location. I rolled up the sack and placed it upon the floor, before gently gripping the head on either side and lifting it. It felt surprisingly heavy and I almost added even more indignity to the man's demise by dropping it. Fortunately I was able to retain my hold upon it as I placed it inside of the sack. It was with a significant degree of relief that I was able to close up the sack, therefore hiding its contents from my gaze.

I continued in the same vain with the remaining two heads, pausing for a while as I looked down at the grey haired man's face. It had already taken on a different appearance. I wondered quite what the people left on the other side of the gateway would be making of what'd happened. How they would cope with being presented with three headless bodies where mere minutes ago they were three happily drunken men, perhaps having finished their work for the day and deciding to take a few drinks in the local pub. Perhaps they were celebrating something of note in their lives, or perhaps this was simply their daily existence.

As I wrapped this last man's head in the sack, I took a final moment to contemplate their fate before picking all three sacks up, for this is what they'd already become in my mind, and carried them through the tunnel and into the barn. The Beast seemed to gloat over their presence, as if proving its power beyond all doubt, if there ever had been any such thing.

It would have been impossible for any onlookers to have known what was inside of the bundle of sacking that I now carried over my shoulder, but I still felt the need for caution before stepping out into the world with my guilty load. There was no one to be seen of course, and so I carried them as swiftly as I could into the large potting shed that sat at the rear of the property. It smelt musky and unused, with a faint odour of soil in the background. I had to clear the bench of its contents before I could manoeuvre the coffin into place from where I found it, leaning into the corner as it had been for many years. I didn't spend too much time in cleaning it down, anxious as I was to rid myself of the sacks and their contents. When I hefted each of the heads into the coffin, I was careful to lay them down gently, as if anxious not to upset the spirits of those that had once inhabited them. They looked odd, lying side by side in the coffin. I paused in thought for a while, feeling the urge to say something meaningful before closing the lid. When nothing would come to mind, I slowly pulled the coffin lid into place. The finality of it dropping into position lifted the weight that had been upon me the whole time, but not entirely.

It seemed prudent to ensure that if curious eyes were laid upon the coffin, that it should at least be temporarily fixed down, and so I spent the next few minutes hammering a half dozen nails into the wood, with every thud of the hammer reminding me of how the heads had thudded dully onto the floor. I was relieved to leave the coffin behind as I closed the door and walked slowly back to the house.

I found the Professor still in the basement. He'd cleaned up what little evidence there was of the awful event, and was now standing in front of his instruments gazing thoughtfully down.

'I've placed them in the coffin, Professor,' I announced, my voice sounding strained. 'What should we do now?'

'Do now? William, as much as this incident pains me I feel there is little choice but to move forward, don't you?'

'But, Professor, three men have died today. How can we simply continue as if nothing has happened?'

'We cannot, William, but we can also not halt our work. Scientific endeavours cannot be allowed to wither because of one tragic accident. I feel for those men, of course, but would we not be inflicting a disservice upon them were their deaths have been for nothing.'

'This technology is dangerous, Professor. People have died. How many more will die if we continue. At least let's involve some additional manpower. Another scientist who can offer some assistance that might prevent any such happenings reoccurring.'

I knew as soon as the words had escaped me that the Professor would react badly to such a thing, but I still didn't expect such an impassioned response as was the case.

'ANOTHER SCIENTIST! Are you trying to give away my work, William? Are you truly suggesting that I allow another to share my invention? My goodness, William, you shock me.'

'I only meant to suggest that we—'

71

'That we what, William? And whom may I ask were you thinking of? Professor Doolan, perhaps? Has your fiance had anything to do with your thoughts upon the matter?'

'Ruthie is not my fiance, Professor, and no, she has not.'

'Then why would you suggest such a thing?'

I looked about the basement in desperation, unable to articulate my thoughts as I kept seeing those heads falling in front of me. The life draining away from a man who had no explanation for what had happened to him. It was too much. How could I carry on with my involvement now that innocent lives had been lost.

'I ... I do not think I can continue, Professor. Not now. Not after this.'

The Professor realised that my continued involvement was teetering on the brink of collapse. That the young man he'd mentored all of these years was on the verge of turning his back upon him, or at least his work. Which I suppose to the Professor was one and the same thing.

'I cannot stop now, William. I cannot. I owe it to the world to continue in my work. My god, William, it works. It really works, and we've both seen it with our own eyes.'

I could not think clearly enough just then to make a decision. The weight of what had happened was too much to bear for such a young mind I think. I looked at him as if seeing him for the first time. He was lost to his work and nothing I could say would change his mind, either with continuing or on the idea of bringing in additional scientific assistance. I found myself shaking my head, not really knowing what I would do.

'I need to take some air, Professor. I need to ... consider

what is right.'

'What is right, William, is that you fulfil your obligations as my assistant.'

I could not speak any further on the subject, and despite his stern gaze, I turned about and left him there, not knowing where I was going or what I would do.

I suspect in reality I knew where I would go just then, but I wish I hadn't. At first I simply left the house and walked aimlessly, but before too long I looked up and realised I was only two streets away from Ruthie's house. It was predictable, I suppose, but I still felt an element of surprise within.

As I walked those last two streets to her door, I tried to imagine what I would say, if anything. How could I reveal the Professor's work to her? How could I possibly confess that I'd witnessed three men dying in such a horrific accident? Could I trust her not to tell her father? Of course, I quickly pushed the question of trust from my mind, or at least as far from it as I could. It did not bode well for our future relationship if I felt a lack of trust in Ruthie, and in a way it felt as though I was undermining one of the two most important aspects of my life. The Professor and my Ruthie.

Chapter Thirteen

I stood outside of Ruthie's house for a while, wondering whether it would be better to take myself somewhere else. I hardly knew what to say to her. My head was spinning. I was being constantly availed of visions of the accident, making me feel nauseas and light-headed. Eventually I simply felt too weak in body and mind to do anything other than seek her counsel, or at the very least, her calming presence.

I'd quite forgotten about my near encounter with Morris as our intruder had fled the barn that previous day, and as the door swung inward and I was met by his presence, I experienced a confusion as I felt myself to be consorting with a potential enemy.

'Master Winn,' he greeted me formally and I don't know if it were simply my over-active imagination, but I fancied his eyes narrowed as he studied me with a modicum of suspicion behind that steely gaze of his. 'Please, come in.'

'Is Ruthie available? I'd like to call upon her,' I said, unable to meet his eye as I entered. The sounds of the street disappeared as the door was closed, and I was left with the silence between us.

'I will enquire whether Miss Doolan is available. Would you care to wait in the drawing room?'

'Thank you, Morris.' Something about the way he phrased this made me uneasy. I allowed myself to be shown into the drawing room, feeling the man's eyes upon me as he slowly closed the door. It was a relief to be out of his company.

I was unable to settle, and rather than taking a seat I found myself walking about the room, looking yet not seeing the contents as I thought back upon recent events. As I reached the windows that looked out upon the garden, I felt a wave of emotion flood through me.

'William, what's wrong?'

I heard my Ruthie's voice as if from a great distance. I hadn't even realised I'd sank to the floor, my body giving way under the sheer weight of my emotions. As I looked around as if discovering where I was for the first time, I saw her rushing forth to comfort me. I was embarrassed by my show of weakness yet unable to put a stop to it.

Her soothing presence calmed me after a time and I was at last able to place myself upon the couch in a more dignified manner.

'What is it, William? Tell me,' she demanded with concern etched upon her face. 'What has happened?'

I told her then. I knew even as the words spilled from me in an uncontrolled rush of feeling and emotion, that I should not have told all, but the look in her eyes and the touch of her hand was enough to undo any contrivance on my part to hold back the truth. I saw her eyes grow wide with wonder and a questioning look appear upon her face, but when I told of the fate of the three unfortunate men that had been drawn through natural curiosity to peer through the Gateway, that look turned to one of shock and horror. A horror that reflected my own feelings at the time. My sense of that moment was becoming dulled as time allowed for some mental recovery on my part, but I knew it would never leave me entirely.

'What are you going to do now, William?' She asked, her face having turned a whiter shade than was usual. 'Will you inform the authorities? Will the Professor bring to an end such reckless experimentations?'

'To what end would we inform any authorities, Ruthie? We don't know where these fellows are from. It was a tragic accident indeed, but we have no mechanism with which to make things right.' To my own surprise I heard myself taking an almost identical viewpoint as the Professor. 'And to abandon such work. Work that can ... no, *will* revolutionise the very world that we live in. Well, it would simply be another tragedy in its own way, don't you think?'

Ruthie sat back, breathing so hard that I thought for a moment she may faint. Then, as her breathing slowed she took on an altogether more purposeful appearance.

'We must tell my father, William. He'll know what to do for the best. Apparently there've been questions asked at The Association regarding Professor Thorebourne and his ... state of mind. My father said that he was not himself at their last meeting.'

'No.' My instant refusal manifested itself in a rather more austere manner to which I'd intended. 'We cannot involve your father. You heard of his reaction when I suggested we involve another, and besides, there is another reason that I must insist that he is not informed of any of this, Ruthie.'

'Another reason? What reason, William?'

'There was ... an incident, several days ago.' I pondered whether I should in fact tell her of what had come to pass, but it seemed I had already left all discretion behind. 'It was the day that the Professor attended The Association's offices at your father's invite. I caught a man snooping about our property, looking for something, it would appear.'

'And what has that to do with my father?' She asked somewhat tersely.

'I chased the man away. He escaped, but not before I saw him getting into a carriage. There was another man already inside and I'm certain it was your father's man, Morris.' In fact I was still unconvinced that it was him, but something spurred me on to assert what I thought I'd seen at the time.

'Morris? That's absurd, William. Why on earth would Morris be involved in such a thing?' She huffed her derision as she got to her feet, pacing the room in annoyance. 'What exactly are you implying, William?'

'I ... I don't know, Ruthie, really I don't, but you have to admit that it doesn't look good.'

'What are you saying? How dare you imply that my father would involve himself in some kind of subterfuge. He is a respected member of The Association *and* a gentleman.'

She locked eyes upon me in a fury that was entirely unfamiliar. I saw then that there would be no understanding forthcoming of my plight, or indeed any degree of openness to the unseemly possibilities that I had lain before her.

'I shouldn't have come, Ruthie. Please forgive me. I would ask again that you do not convey any of this to your father. I am sure that I am mistaken and that I've spoken out of turn.'

'I am certain of it!'

Ruthie's unforgiving stare was as much a dismissal as I could expect. I repeated my apologies and left her with one last plea not to inform her father of what had taken place. I felt like I had betrayed the Professor's trust, and also Ruthie's. I began to question my own version of events. In my mind's eye the sight of Morris half hidden within the shadows of the carriage became more blurred and indistinct. I wondered if the Professor's paranoia had infected my own mind. Whether I was seeing plots and conspiracies where none truly existed.

I left the house feeling even more distraught than I had beforehand. As I began once more my aimless wandering about the streets, I began to question just how far Ruthie would heed my pleas. I wished I felt that her loyalty to me would prevent her from revealing the truth to Professor Doolan, but something told me that I would be disappointed - both in her and myself.

I resolved to return home. To face the Professor and try to reason with him once more, knowing in my heart that the outcome would likely remain unchanged.

Chapter Fourteen

My reluctance to face the Professor knowing that I'd done precisely what he'd asked me not to, did not stop the rising sense of urgency I felt in returning to the house. There was a growing and pervasive sense of panic inside of me that I'd ruined everything. That Professor Doolan would simply alert the authorities and bring them down upon us for the deaths of the three men, and in doing so, find his way to taking charge of the Professor's most groundbreaking scientific project in his lifetime, if not the lifetimes of us all.

I swallowed my anxieties and stepped inside the house with an overwhelming sense of guilt. I should have stood by the Professor, or at the very least debated the crisis further rather than turn my back upon him. Stopping in the hallway, I listened for signs of the Professor moving about the house, but there was nothing. I knew where he'd be but I guess I was delaying the time where I'd have to confront him with my weakness.

The door to the basement was still open as I reached it, much as it had been when I'd left. I doubted the man had even left the room in his obsession to overcome the latest issues. As I made my way slowly downward I became aware of the incessant mutterings of a man obsessed. He was quite unaware of my presence as I stood there at the bottom of the steps, watching him scribbling profusely in his notebook.

'Professor?' I waited for him to realise that someone had spoken before continuing. 'I must offer my apologies, Sir.' His back straightened and then he turned, a lack of recognition upon his face for several moments before he focused upon my face.

'Apologies? Whatever for, William?'

'My ... My behaviour, Professor. I should never have left—'

'Don't be absurd, William. You're quite right to be in shock at what has happened. Quite right, indeed. I knew you'd be back.' He sighed then, a sigh of such burden that I immediately felt sorry for the man. 'We'll take some time to mourn this evening. To say a few words and express our own grief at what has happened, but right now I have a thought that I must share with my most valuable assistant.' His smile was so warm that I wondered how I could ever have turned my back upon him. My guilt festered beneath the surface as I struggled with my inevitable confession.

'But, Professor, there's something I must tell—'

'Not now, William. Now you must listen and tell me what you think.' He briefly turned back to his notes before fixing me with an inquisitive look. 'I'm almost certain that I heard what I believe to be Northern accents through the Gateway before it was ... shut down. I've studied the effects of the Earth's own magnetic fields upon the Gateway's electromagnetic field and I'm convinced that it's being drawn toward the North's magnetic pole. If this is so, I would propose that by increasing the power levels we would push the portal further North, and we could in fact avoid any populated areas by doing so.' He drifted off for several seconds as he considered his own plans. I knew it was useless to address any response to him at this time, and so I waited for him to return. He did so with a flourish. 'As long as the Gateway can be kept stable over such a distance, I see no reason why this would not work. Do you, William?'

'Um, no, Professor, I suppose not.' It didn't seem to be a great leap from where we were now and I had little reason to think this would present any additional issues. 'But before we do so, there's one thing I need to—'

'Not now, William. I wish to proceed as soon as possible. Run up to the house and bring us back our coats. We may find it somewhat cooler in the North, don't you think?'

'We'll be going through this time, Professor?' The idea unnerved me, I shall admit.

'Indeed. Despite the ... end result, we've proved the Gateway to be stable enough to allow human travel, have we not? We'll exercise some degree of caution, of course, but I see no reason to forestall our next steps.'

He ushered me from the basement then, wanting to proceed as quickly as possible. I was annoyed at myself for not telling him what I'd done, knowing that at some point it would inevitably come back to haunt me. As I retrieved the coats from the hallway I hurried back, trying to rationalise my reluctance to confess my indiscretions but with little success.

Chapter Fifteen

'Good, William. Now, please start up the engine whilst I make some final calculations. It would not do to find ourselves stepping through only to find ourselves in outer-space!'

'Outer-space? Do you think that could happen, Professor?' The shock was evidently upon my face as he laughed at me.

'It is conceivable, I admit, although I've hypothesised that in order to achieve an atomic magnetic attraction through space it would still require an equal volume of atomic matter on the other side. This would seem to exclude the possibility of a portal forming in empty space, although I confess I cannot say whether the machine is capable of reaching other planets. Do not worry, William. We will not be using enough power to risk such a thing. I am quite certain that I can apply such an increase in power that would restrict the connection to our very own planet.'

I swallowed hard as my mind focused on the idea of appearing upon a distant world. I wondered what Saturn or Mars would be like if I were to step through and find myself upon them, and quickly turned away from such thoughts lest I lose all sense of purpose.

Once the engine was brought into motion and the steam had begun to thrust the great arm up and down via the piston, I scurried back to the basement. The Professor it seemed had completed his checks and had turned the control dial up to a degree that we had not attempted before. I watched over his shoulder as the power levels rose and we both donned our ear dampeners and hats with goggles at the ready. As the noise level rose and the floor hummed with the power of The Beast, the Professor switched on the feedback loop and the power level began to increase rapidly once more. My very insides trembled as I anticipated actually accompanying the Professor through the Gateway.

'Are you ready, William?' The Professor called to me, a look of excitement in his eyes.

I nodded, trying to emulate his enthusiasm but unable to do so. I nodded emphatically, hoping this would suffice. Seeing him pull his goggles down over his eyes, I did the same, feeling that I was about to embark upon a great adventure, and fearing the very same. The switch was thrown and the power output released upon the Gateway. A blinding flash of light - or it would have been if not for the eye protection - lit up the basement, and then the Gateway was once more alive in front of us.

The Professor picked up the wooden pole as if handling something more technical than the most basic of items, and stepped forward, lance in hand. As before, he thrust it slowly but surely into the light, moving closer and closer as no resistance was felt. I could feel the temperature beginning to drop about us as the cold air on the other side invaded our own space. Having successfully sent almost the entire length of the pole through the portal, the Professor now withdrew, shrugging his shoulders as the cold air began to bite.

'It is clear, William. Let us don our coats and prepare.'

I gratefully pulled my coat on, with the addition of a scarf that I'd also brought with me. I eyed the Gateway nervously, but despite my worries I could not quell the excited anticipation of being one of the first people in history to pass through an Interspacial Gateway. I flashed back to the sight of three heads dropping to the floor for a moment, before taking control of myself once more.

The Professor approached the Gateway and listened for a while, seeming satisfied that he could hear no signs of people on the other side.

'I will go first, William. Be ready to shut down the Gate should anything go wrong. If there is danger, I will return swiftly. If not, I will still return quite soon to you, and then you may follow.'

'Should we not ensure that there is always one person on this side, Professor?' I asked, feeling this to be a sensible precaution, although what I expected to be achieved by one of us closing down the Gateway and possibly stranding the other upon the other side, I do not know.

The Professor thought over this point, and despite not appearing entirely convinced that it was necessary, nodded, saying, 'Yes, that may be sensible, William. We will take it in turns to explore the other side. Wish me luck, William. Wish me luck!'

'Good luck, Professor,' I said, and then with one final nod between us, he faced the light and walked through.

I was at first shocked at how wilfully he'd taken himself into the light, thinking that he would at least have passed an arm or a leg through, but it seemed he was determined to take the plunge

84

on this occasion. He put the courage of his own convictions first and disappeared from view.

I stared after him. Looking into the light as I waited with bated breath for him to reappear, my worse fears rising within me as I wondered whether I would ever see him again. Time passed slowly. It was a most tortuous wait as I cast my gaze over the control panel every so often, checking that everything appeared stable, or at least as well as I could estimate. I suddenly felt perfectly inadequate to be standing over the controls, knowing that the one person who truly understood the phenomena was now at its very mercy, in a place I knew not.

I checked my watch, recalling the day the Professor had given it to me. It'd been his since a young age, and as I turned fifteen years old, he'd decided I should have a watch of my own. My fondness and respect for the man swelled within me and I was within a hair's breadth of plunging into the light after him, when I detected a familiar rippling effect and then he was there once more, stepping back through, looking none the worse for wear.

'Professor!' I could simply not contain my joy at seeing him again. It was all I could do to restrain myself from running to him for a hug as I would once have done as a young boy. My relief was enormous. 'You did it, Professor. You did it!'

'Why, yes, William. I did indeed.'

'What's on the other side? Where has the Gateway taken you to?' My joy at seeing him alive was being swiftly overtaken by curiosity at what lay beyond the light. I was no longer nervous of passing through. I was now desperate to experience the Professor's Interspacial Gateway for myself. He shuddered as I noticed his red nose and cheeks flushed from the cold.

'I believe I was correct in my calculations. It has indeed

been directed further into the north. Given the position of the sun and the temperature I would say that it's positioned inside of the Arctic Circle, however, it is not located where I had expected.'

'Where is it then, Professor?'

'Well, I suspect it has somehow passed over the magnetic pole and emerged upon the opposite side to where we are. Whether there is a random element being introduced into its course or whether it is more associated with the power levels being used, I cannot say. This phenomena will require further examination.'

'Is it safe, Professor?'

'Mmm, what's that?'

'Is it safe, Professor, for me to pass through?'

'Oh, I see. Oh yes, William, quite safe. I will remain here, it is only fitting that you should experience our results for yourself, but do not stray far from the Gateway, William, and do not dally too long. Shall we say five minutes for this first venture?'

'Five minutes,' I agreed, wrapping my scarf tightly about myself.

I stepped up to the light, having to squint through the goggles at such close proximity. Unable to bring myself to simply step through as the Professor had done, I thrust my hand into the unknown, feeling the chill beyond the gateway biting into me. As I withdrew my arm I looked down upon my fingers, wiggling them about to eradicate the numbing cold. With one final deep breath, I gathered myself up and urged myself forward. It was a strange experience, passing through that Gateway for the first time. The light was so intense that I closed my eyes for a moment, and it felt as though my body was momentarily pulled forward before being almost pushed out the other end. The hairs on the back of my neck prickled furiously as I opened my eyes and was presented with the wilderness beyond.

The air was icy cold. The landscape bleak and uninviting. I looked behind me to see the portal still there, framed by a mountainous vista beyond. I was near to a shoreline, its edges fringed with grey rocks and a sparse vegetation. The water itself was an iron grey colour which closely matched the sky above. The shock of being transported into such a cold environment caused me to shiver. As I breathed in the crisp air I could barely believe where I was - where I'd come from. It was incomprehensible that such a thing had been made possible, yet the Professor had made it so.

Looking around I could see birds on the ground in the distance but no people. The Professor's words came back to me, and I had thoughts of stepping straight back into the light lest I be stranded, but I needed to walk about. To prove to myself that this was not a dream. That I really did have the frozen ground beneath my feet and the deep northern ocean in front. I could feel myself becoming chilled as I walked slowly away from the safety of my only way home, but still I continued. I clambered over a rock formation and below me the ground dropped away into a gully where seabirds gathered in great numbers. They called as if to protest my presence in their untouched land. It was astonishing.

It was tempting to keep going, but the wind was cutting into me despite my coat - which was not intended for such frozen climes. With one final look around at this distant and unknown location, I walked briskly back up the incline, my courage fading as I imagined what it would be like to be left there should the Gateway fail. Would the Professor be able to reopen it in the same place or close by? I didn't know, and I was loath to find out whilst on this side.

As I stepped back through and experienced the same pulling and pushing sensations assault me, I emerged with a triumphant smile upon my face and some degree of relief inside of me.

'What do you say, William?' The Professor asked as he shut down the Gateway behind me. Immediately the cold air was cut off and I was relieved to feel the relative warmth of the basement envelop me.

'It's incredible, Professor. I was in a different location entirely. The world will be transformed by your work. Wait until the Association and the Royal Society hear of this. You'll be famous, Professor. The talk of London.'

'Not yet, William. We have more work to do to ensure that it is stable and that the results can be replicated. We must carry out a full check of the apparatus before carrying out more tests.'

He was right of course, but there was reason why I now felt an impatience to tell the world. If the Professor went public before Ruthie could break my confidence and inform her father, then my indiscretion would no longer be an issue for us - or rather, for *me*.'

Chapter Sixteen

A thorough check of the apparatus followed, whereby we ensured everything was in working order and there were no signs of any pending failures. It was frustrating at times as all I could think of was to venture once more through the Gateway and experience a distant land. I was most impressed by how the Professor himself held onto his own enthusiasms, choosing to attend to his work in a most diligent and methodical manner.

When finally it seemed that there was no stone left unturned in our quest to find anything out of place, we gathered ourselves in the dining room for some much needed sustenance. Mrs Hill had kindly provided for us, and with her usual flawless discretion left us to discuss our work alone.

'Well, my boy, we're ready to prepare our expedition.'

'Expedition, Professor?'

'Yes, indeed. We'll treat every journey through the Gateway as such and therefore ensure that we're properly prepared for any eventuality. We'll start by gathering some appropriate arctic clothing. We may be spending more time exposed to such conditions as we document our proof.'

'Will we need to document it whilst on the other side, Professor?'

'It is my intention, William, to provide irrefutable and overwhelming evidence of the successful working of the Gateway. We'll be including photographic images from the other side of the Gateway itself and its surroundings. We'll also attempt to bring back some samples of the environment in order to support the photographs themselves.'

'But Professor, what proof will we have that any of this has been obtained by ourselves, and not simply purchased from those that have made such journey's by ship?'

'The photographs will be evidence enough, William, I'm sure of it. We'll take the day's papers through with us and pose with them. Then, when we present the evidence it will be obvious that we could not have possibly undertaken such an expedition and returned to England so swiftly as to make a false claim.' The Professor got to his feet, his hands clasped behind his back as he walked the room. 'It is my intention to present my paper to the Royal Society first. I will not give Professor Doolan the opportunity to peruse my work until it has been accredited and witnessed by others beyond his spere of influence.'

Despite knowing the history of the two men and my suspicions regarding Professor Doolan and his man, Morris, this still felt like a somewhat paranoid approach to me, however, it was the Professor's decision to make. I could only imagine the numerous noses of the Association members being put out of their respective joints when they discovered that one of their own had sought out the support of the Royal Society over themselves.

The Professor brought down to the basement his camera,

complete with tripod, and readied it for being taken through the gate. I myself was tasked with gathering more suitable clothing for an arctic expedition. We were not intending to stay for more than two or three hours at most, but depending on the severity of the weather we encountered, this could still be enough time for a man to freeze to death in such conditions.

Once we'd gathered enough equipment to make it appear as though we were indeed heading off on a month long trek to the Arctic, the Professor turned to me, all of a fluster.

'What is it, Professor?' I asked, immediately concerned that something serious had occurred to him that could jeopardise our trip.

'The papers, William, the papers!' He rifled through his pockets before thrusting a handful of coins upon me. 'Quickly, William, go fetch the day's papers. We must have them.'

I looked at him with some relief as I realised the expedition wasn't in danger, although "expedition" did seem a somewhat grand description of what we were about to undertake. His anxiousness caused me to flee the basement as if my heels were on fire. I raced to the local paper seller and after a brief consideration, I collected up an armful of papers and hurriedly payed for them. In my angst to get away I feel I must have left a rather generous tip behind, as the man doffed his cap most gratefully whilst holding a hand full of coins out in surprise.

All was ready upon my return and we added the papers to the contents of a small case that contained the camera's glass slides. It was then that a worrying thought struck me and I wondered why we hadn't spoken of it before.

'Professor, are we safe leaving the controls unattended with us both on the other side?'

'I believe we are, William, but to ensure that all remains well I will intermittently return through the Gateway and determine if there are any problems. I've affixed a red flag to the pole. If you see this come through the Gateway whilst I am on the other side you must follow me through at once leaving all of the equipment behind.' I nodded solemnly as I saw the square of red material that he'd tied upon the pole. 'I do not believe there will be a problem as long as the engine is able to sustain the necessary power output to maintain a stable Gateway. Do not look so worried, William, all will be well.'

I wasn't aware that I had been wearing such a worried expression. I forced a grin in response.

Chapter Seventeen

'Right, William. We'll initiate the Gateway and then I'll pass through first. I'll come back for you and the equipment once I've had a look at our location. I've not changed the power settings so I'm hopeful we will at least be in the vicinity of our last position.'

The Beast was fired up and we waited impatiently for the power levels to rise. As the feedback loop was thrown open I looked over at the Professor nervously, knowing that this could be the point that the Professor's work was finally revealed to the world.

I'm sure it was my imagination, but the Gateway seemed to light up even brighter than before, as if it knew of the importance of this expedition. We shared a look through darkened goggles, both wearing our top hats as if expecting the Queen herself to be waiting on the other side. Then the Professor walked through and I saw the ripples ebb and flow behind him.

I stepped to the control panel and was pleased to see that nothing appeared out of place. The sound of the engine emanating down the communication tunnel surrounded me, even so, I heard another sound that did not quite fit for a moment. I strained to listen and through the noise of the machine I was able to make out the high pitched tinkling of a bell. There was someone at the front door. For a moment I was torn. Those imprinted manners dictated that I leave the basement and enquire as to who was calling, yet I hardly dared leave the controls. As it rang again I reasoned that I was of little use where I was, and that a momentary absence would likely not have any noticeable affect. The Professor was likely to be some time as I imagined him trudging around the immediate area of the Gateway, looking for signs of people and trying to estimate how close he was to the previous location.

With one last check of the controls, I hurried from my station and up the stairs, intent on sending whoever the caller was away until a more convenient time. As I reached the doorway at the top of the stairs I stepped out in a hurry, quite forgetting that I was still wearing my protective equipment.

A darkened silhouette was in the hallway and I rebuked myself mentally for not locking the door properly. It took only a moment or two to recognise Ruthie even through my goggles, and judging by her startled look I guessed I must have made for quite an unexpected sight.

'Ruthie!' I called, stopping in my tracks to pull down my goggles and ear dampeners. 'What are you doing here?'

'William, what are you wearing? And what's that awful sound?'

'Oh, it's just ... we're in the middle of an experiment.' I approached swiftly, my joy at seeing my darling conflicting with the need to return to the basement. 'It's ... It's not a good time, I'm afraid.'

'Well, when is a good time, William? I hardly see you these days, and since you told me of your work with the Professor you've not been near.'

'I'm sorry, Ruthie.' I could see her anger, but behind it lurked something else. A discomfort in her eyes that told me all was not entirely well. 'What is it? What's wrong, Ruthie?'

'Does something have to be wrong for me to call upon you?'

'No, of course not, it's just that—'

'Where's the Professor?'

'The Professor? He's ... He's in the basement. I should go back to him really. I'm sorry that—'

'I'd like to speak with him.'

'That's not poss—' She pushed my hands away and marched passed me. For a moment I wasn't sure what she was doing, but then she headed directly toward the open basement door and I called to her in surprise. 'NO! Ruthie, you can't—'

'I can and I will,' she said, hurrying forward as I struggled to catch up with her.

Once she was negotiating the stairs there was little I could do to stop her. She pressed her hands to her ears as she reached the bottom, looking around her for the source of the noise. As her eyes settled upon the Gateway, she stopped. She was trying to simultaneously shield her eyes and her ears as she squinted in wonder at the bright light of the Interspatial Gateway. I quickly retrieved some spare equipment and placed the ear dampeners over her ears before handing her a pair of goggles. She looked at them in confusion for a moment before taking off her hat and pulling them over her head. She made for an odd sight, standing there in her crinoline dress, lace gloves and thick dark goggles, her hair tussled from pulling off her hat.

'So it's true. All you said about this ... *doorway* to another place,' she said, not taking her eyes off the Gateway.

'Yes. Did you not believe me?' I asked.

'Yes, I suppose I did. It's just that my father said that such a thing would be quite—'

'Your father? Please tell me you didn't talk to him of this, Ruthie?'

'I didn't mean to exactly. He was concerned that—'

'RUTHIE! I told you not to say anything,' I snapped at her in a most ungentlemanly manner. I could see the hurt in her face but this was quickly supplanted by anger.

'William Winn, how dare you speak to me in such a way! I've been worried about you. Who else could I have spoken to of such a thing. My father can help, William. With his help you can—'

'Can what, Ruthie? The Professor doesn't need his help, and I told you what happened with the intruder. With Morris.'

'And this is the Gateway?'

Her sudden change of subject threw me. It would have been obvious to her that it was, but she needed my confirmation anyway. I looked at the Gateway too and I was struck with its wonder as if seeing it for the very first time.

'Yes, Ruthie, it is. The Professor's on the other side now. He'll be back soon.'

'How soon?'

'I ... I don't know. Why?'

'Because my father's on his way here, and he means to uncover the Professor's work for himself.'

'But, he has no right to. This is Professor Thorebourne's work. *His* house. He has no right!' I couldn't believe what she was saying to me, and I was at a lost as to what to do.

'My father says that it is dangerous. That it needs a more cautious approach.'

My thoughts drifted to the three heads that rested inside the Professor's coffin. If only she knew what grotesque misfortune they'd been met with, she would be even more adamant that we allow her father to become involved in our work.

'Professor Thorebourne will never agree. You can't do this. You must tell your father not to come.'

I knew as I looked at her that she would not do this. That her father was a far more fearful prospect than either myself or Professor Thorebourne.

'I must see. I must see what's on the other side.' She stepped closer to the Gateway, hugging herself against the chill air.

'No, you cannot, Ruthie. I'm sorry, but I cannot allow you to go through.'

It was as if she hadn't heard me, or maybe she did and that's why she suddenly walked forward, striding bravely into the Gateway. I should have stopped her. I should have expected such a thing and placed myself between her and the Gate, but I did not.

'RUTHIE!' It was too late. She was already gone, the surface of the Gateway rippling in her wake as if to taunt me.

97

I was caught in a dilemma. Her father was apparently on his way to the house yet I was desperate to follow her. She was not dressed for the cold that she would find on the other side. I looked from the Gateway to the basement stairs and back again.

I let out a cry of frustration before quickly gathering what warm clothing I could. I hoped the Professor had been somewhere close by, so that he may see Ruthie coming through the gate and guide her back to the safety of the basement. I hesitated for several seconds, watching the gate as I expected either one or both to reappear at any time, but they did not. There was little choice but to follow in the hope that we could all return before Ruthie's father was upon us.

Chapter Eighteen

I felt the rather disconcerting sensation of being first pulled and then pushed through the Gateway before appearing on the other side. I did not expect what I found and it explained why the Professor had still not returned through the Gateway.

The portal had opened upon some kind of rock field. I felt my left foot step onto a smooth surface and then I was losing my balance and falling forwards. I threw the bundle of thick clothing in front of me and I'm convinced this alone saved me from injury. Nevertheless, I landed hard. The unforgiving rocks beneath me knocked the very breath from my lungs. As I tried to suck in air I was assaulted by the freezing temperatures about me. The weather was considerably worse than the first expedition and I wondered vaguely whether we were in an entirely different location to that first one.

Having forced several deep breaths despite the cold air, I called out about me. 'RUTHIE? PROFESSOR?' The wind took my words instantly and I cast my eyes around at the uneven piles of rocks about me. I thought I heard something close by, and hoping beyond hope, I scrambled to the top of a jagged rise next to me and looked over. There, at the bottom of a dip in the rocks lay Ruthie. 'RUTHIE!' I shouted, before climbing down toward her. I was already freezing cold and as I reached her unmoving body, I dragged a coat over her prone form before donning my own. 'Ruthie, are you hurt?' It was clear that she was. She'd managed somehow to fall down the treacherous slope of rocks and now her very life may have been in danger.

I felt her brow. It felt as cold as the rocks she was lying upon. I shook her gently and much to my relief heard a moan escape her lips. 'Ruthie, can you hear me?' I pleaded, wondering where the Professor had gotten to. Had the same fate befallen him too? Was he lying nearby in a similar predicament as Ruthie?

I bent close to her ear and was able to see her lips moving. I could barely hear her above the gusting winds above. 'Stay still, Ruthie. I'm going to get you back to the basement.' Despite my claims, I had no idea just how I would manage such a feat on my own. I had to find the Professor and hope that he was still able to assist. Ruthie's life very well depended upon getting her back to the basement.

I covered her up as best I could and made my way to the top of the nearest rock pile, looking about in desperation. 'PROFESSOR?' I shouted. 'PROFESSOR THOREBOURNE?' I'm not certain why I shouted his name like that. It's unlikely that another Professor in the vicinity would have mistaken my calls. It was just as I was about to clamber back down in a desperate attempt to carry Ruthie to safety on my own that I saw him, waving at me from a good fifty feet away. I beckoned to him, relief washing through me until I looked down and saw Ruthie lying quite still upon the rocks.

It was an interminable wait for the Professor to reach me. The rocks were perilous to navigate and I lost sight of him for a moment as he entered a dip, before once again appearing. I took hold of his arm and helped steady him over the last couple of feet.

'Professor,' I shouted into his ear. 'Ruthie is hurt. She came through the Gateway and has fallen.' I pointed below us as I realised he hadn't seen her underneath the large coat. His mouth dropped open and he looked at me questioningly. Any explanations would have to wait, I decided, and leaned in once more. 'We have to get her back to the basement.' The Professor nodded his head, concern etched into his face as we each steadied one another on the descent.

I moved to her head, forcing my hands underneath her in order to lift her up under the shoulders. The Professor took her legs and between us we hefted her up into the air. She screamed then. A high pitched cry of agony as her broken body was manhandled. The coat was still draped over her but I knew she would be vulnerable to the cold, yet there was little we could do in our current position. We struggled to get her out of the dip and came to a rest at the top. Ruthie cried out each time we moved her and I was forced to harden my heart to her grief. We managed to wrap her in the coat more effectively and the Professor gave up his fur hat to keep her warm. She looked deathly pale. Her lips bloodless and blue.

We both contemplated the hazardous path back to the Gateway and the Professor pointed out what appeared the easiest route. It was not far, but I knew it would be a torment.

Gathering our strength we heaved her up into the air once more amidst her terrible cries of pain and anguish. I tried to reassure her with some words of encouragement, but I knew she could barely hear me and the effort was too much to continue.

She swayed between us as we stumbled our way to the Gate. I looked up from Ruthie's face to see the doorway almost within reach, and then - nothing.

I stopped where I was, not understanding what had happened. Where a second ago there was the bright light of the Gateway, now there was just the continuing vista of the rock field beyond.

It had gone.

The Gateway had closed.

Chapter Nineteen

'Professor.' I continued to stare dumbfounded. 'PROFESSOR!'

The Professor looked up, seeing my face he turned to look behind him where only moments ago the Gateway had been. He appeared as stunned as I was at first.

'Where ... Where is the Gate?' He asked.

We lowered Ruthie to the floor, neither of us knowing quite what to do.

'It's closed, Professor. I think ... I think maybe someone closed it from the other side,' I said. 'We must get Ruthie to shelter. Out of this wind.' The reminder of the biting wind howling about us was enough to jolt him back out of our predicament. 'Did you notice anywhere we could shelter as you explored?'

'Why, yes, William. I believe I did. Over there, below that escarpment there is shelter, and further on I believe I saw what appeared to be a whaling station or some such settlement. It didn't appear inhabited but you never know.'

'We must go, quickly!'

'Oh, yes, quite so, my boy. Quite so. This way, It's easier once we're over that rise.'

We struggled to carry Ruthie with us, yet neither of us even once thought to leave her behind of course. The Professor was right. After clambering up and down the rocks for another hundred feet or so we were able to navigate a smoother path where the rocks turned to a kind of scree. I've no idea how long we spent carrying my beloved. We had to rest several times, and my only confirmation that she was still alive was her cries of pain as we laid her upon the cold hard ground before lifting her up once more.

Finally we reached the escarpment which hung over us, providing some shelter from the elements. We found a cave of sorts. It didn't go far back into the rock, but it was enough to give us some relief from the bite of the wind at least. We tried to make Ruthie as comfortable as possible, as far back into the recess as possible, before we stepped closer to the entrance to talk.

'Professor, I think she's going to die if we don't get her out of here. One of us needs to head to the whaling station to see if we can raise some help.'

'But, the Gateway. It's possible it experienced a power spike of some kind and will reconnect itself once more.'

'No, Professor. I think that it may have been shut down from the other side.'

'How? There's no one else in the basement, is there?'

It sometimes astonished me how the Professor, a man of such intelligence and wit, could be unintentionally obtuse at such times. I told him then of Ruthie. Of how I'd confessed all to her, and how she in turn had confessed all to Professor Doolan. The Professor grew increasingly flustered and annoyed at my revelations, and I couldn't blame him. It was my fault and no one else's.

'I'm sorry, Professor. I really am,' I finished, unable to look up from my boots.

The Professor looked at me and nodded. Once, twice, then a third time. 'Now is not the time, young William. We must find our way out of this predicament one way or another. You must take yourself to the whaling station. You'll be swifter than I for certain. I'll stay with Ruthie. If there is no help available there, then - we are indeed lost.'

I thought then that it unlikely we would survive our ordeal. I should never have told Ruthie, and I should never have followed her through, but I knew I would do exactly the same a second time. Such is the hopelessness of the human condition.

Chapter Twenty

Before I left the relative safety of the cave I checked upon Ruthie. Her leg was badly broken and I suspected she'd broken at least one rib too. Her continued state of unconsciousness was a source of deep concern. It was hard to tear myself away from her side but I had little choice. We needed help and there was only one place to look.

I wrapped myself up tightly against the bitter wind and set off as fast as I dared. Although I was no longer walking amongst the rock field the ground was mostly made up of loose stones. I tried to hold my utter despair at bay as I went, telling myself that we'd find a way out of here. My own thoughts held little conviction.

Every so often I would pause and look back to where I thought the Gateway had been before someone or something had closed it. I hoped that it would reappear and afford us a way home, but there was no sign of it. The fact that it had connected to a different location to our previous venture meant that even if it were reopened, that it would likely reappear somewhere else entirely.

The final descent to the whaling station was a slippery affair. I slid my way down the loose slope, losing my footing at one point and tumbling for several feet before coming to a stop. It's seems silly now, but I remember being glad that there was no one to witness my somewhat literal fall from grace.

My heart sank even further as I reached the station and looked about, seeing little sign of occupation. I located what looked like the main accommodation building and half walked, half ran towards it. The door was up a flight of wooden steps and I climbed them without hesitation, pushing the door open with some relief at the promised respite from the cold. Much to my astonishment and that of those inside, I found myself facing three men about to commence their meal. A lit stove was sending out its glorious heat into the room and I thoughtfully closed the door behind me before turning back to my surprised hosts.

'Who are you?' One of them asked in a rather gruff manner.

'Where the 'ell did you come from?' Asked another.

'Please, I need help. My sweetheart has been hurt rather badly. My companion is with her, sheltering at the side of the slope. We need to get them down here and attend to her.'

I don't know if I really expected the men to jump up and act immediately but my sudden appearance, alongside my claim of having an injured girlfriend and companion in the area was clearly taking time to sink in. All three exchanged confused looks before one of them got to his feet. He fixed me with his sharp blue eyes. A tall man, he spoke from behind an unkempt, shaggy beard.

'I asked who you are,' he said, his mouth barely opening as he spoke.

It was only now that I began to wonder if I'd made a mistake. I had no reason to think that these men would indeed offer their help. In fact, it now occurred to me that they may even be the sort to take advantage of such vulnerable guests so far from civilisation.

'My name is William Winn, Sir,' I said, pulling my hat off and trying not to appear as anxious as I now felt. 'As for how we arrived here, it is a long story I'm afraid, but one I would be most glad to tell once my friends are safely brought down from the slope. I beg you, Sirs, please help us.'

He studied me for a moment, looking as though he were on the verge of more questions before raising an eyebrow at his compatriots.

'Come on then, lads. I dare say it'll be a story worth hearing later. Put your coats on, it would seem we're going for a walk.'

'I'm 'ungry an' all!' Complained the one that was yet to speak, gazing down at his plateful of food before setting it aside somewhat reluctantly. He looked skinny, but something about his wiry frame told me he would be far stronger and more robust than he looked. These men led a hard life, I imagined.

For a moment I too gazed down at the food on this man's plate, wanting something warm inside of me, but aside from its unappetising appearance, I knew there was no time to lose. I pulled my hat back on and led the way from the hut as soon as the three men had donned their own thick coats. The wind was coming directly down the slope at us as we forged our way upward, making the return trek even less pleasant than the first.

I'm pleased to say that my rescuers had enough foresight to bring with them a makeshift stretcher, having questioned me on Ruthie's injuries. It made carrying her back down the slope considerably easier than it had been bringing her over the rock field. The look of relief on the Professor's face when I suddenly appeared at the entrance to the shallow cave was clearly evident. He seemed just as surprised as I had been when he set eyes upon the three men that now accompanied me. Amidst much ado we were able to gently place Ruthie, who was still in a state of unconsciousness, upon the stretcher, before making our way slowly down to the station. The Professor followed as the three men and I carried Ruthie ahead, urging us on and telling us not to wait for him. We had some trouble carrying Ruthie up the steps into the hut, but once inside with the door closed I was able to breathe a sigh of intense relief, only to realise that we were far from being clear of any danger.

Chapter Twenty-One

It was obvious we could do very little for Ruthie in the current environment. There were no medical supplies in the hut and all we could do was try to make her comfortable. The food was quickly warmed up and our new found friends were kind enough to share their meal with us. The men from the whaling station explained that they were awaiting supplies and that it could be several days before they arrived. The station had been damaged during some particularly inclement weather several days before and no whaling ships were expected any time soon. This was clearly not good news.

Thomas, the man in charge of the small crew of the station, and his men Laurence and Jack, tried to help as best they could, but nothing they could say or do was likely to improve Ruthie's prospects. They were fine men, I have to say, and I felt a little ashamed of my earlier doubts over their characters.

As night began to fall I took myself outside in search of solitude. The wind had dropped a little as I stood on the veranda looking down the steps to where the stony shore met the dark grey waters. Seabirds rose and fell along the shoreline, calling as if to mock our situation. I turned to look to the south as the sun was setting, its rays hidden behind a bank of cloud that hung low and menacing in the distance. Another source of light caught my attention, near to the shoreline as best I could tell, to the south of us. I squinted, wondering if it were another settlement that the whalers had failed to mention, or even a boat. As I continued to look at the distant light, I thought it was a light shining out through an open doorway, but I couldn't make out any shapes that would indicate a building. My skin prickled and a chill ran down my spine. Spinning around, I burst back into the hut, causing the Professor to stop in mid sentence as he explained our presence to these men. They did not look particularly convinced by his story.

'The Gateway! I think I can see it, to the South of us.' I ignored the Professor's open-mouthed expression as I turned to Thomas. 'Are there any settlements or buildings to our South? Is there anything that would provide a light source there?'

Thomas frowned, saying, 'No, nothing. The nearest settlement is many miles away.'

'Then, Thomas, can you take a look outside and tell me if you recognise this light source?'

Thomas followed me out of the hut and I immediately pointed out the light. I was relieved that it was still showing, as I had wondered whether it would be gone upon my return, but much to my relief it was not. If anything, it was growing more pronounced as the light about us grew dim.

I could tell from the expression on Thomas' face that he was unsure of where the light was coming from. He shook his head uncertainly as we both squinted into the distance.

'It must be the Gateway. It's reopened, and we must get to it if Ruthie has any chance of surviving,' I said, leaving aside my inner desperation to be away from this inhospitable place.

111

'We're losing the light. It'll be difficult in the dark.'

'We have to try. It's our only hope.'

I was acutely aware of the urgency that now existed. I wasn't certain how far away the light was and I knew it could be closed down at any time. We had to go swiftly.

Thomas himself seemed to realise the need to move fast and he led the way back into the hut. The Professor had joined us and he too could see the light.

'Yes, yes, we must go, William. No time to lose, indeed no,' he muttered under his breath. He didn't seem himself at all. As if the shock of finding himself stranded and the disastrous path we now found ourselves upon had shaken him to the core.

As we wrapped Ruthie up in coats and blankets, I brushed her hair from her face and looked for her breathing. It seemed shallow and a little ragged. I didn't say anything aloud, but the sympathetic looks I received from the others was enough to tell me that they shared my concerns. A desperate dash for salvation was at hand as we manoeuvred her out of the hut and back down the steep steps.

Very little was said as we headed along the shoreline in the direction of the light. It was still there, and every now and then I would notice a shadow pass before it as if others were moving about in front of it. If it were indeed the Gateway, it seemed certain that whoever had closed it had managed to reopen it and they would inevitably feel the need to investigate the other side. I wondered if Professor Doolan had any idea that his daughter were on this side too.

It was a small mercy that the wind had lessoned considerably. The fast fading light did nothing to make our journey easier, and although Thomas and his men had brought lanterns, I asked that they not use them until absolutely necessary. It seemed likely that anyone present about the Gateway would be unaware of our approach and the longer we could hide our presence the better for us, I considered.

I was eager to cover the distance as quickly as possible, and as we worked our way along the shoreline I realised that the Gateway was not as far away as I had first thought.

The closer we came the clearer it was that some activity was present about the Gateway itself. The moon began to cast its light over the proceedings and we were able to approach to within a short distance without being detected. The Gateway was positioned on the opposite side of a small rocky promontory, and we gently placed Ruthie onto the floor in the lee of a large boulder before peering silently toward the light.

To my relief I saw that the light was without doubt that of the Gateway, but to my dismay I could see at least two rather brusque looking gentlemen standing nearby, the one turned towards us familiar to me in the light of the Gateway. I'd seen this man before, when he'd entered the barn before fleeing to board the carriage with whom I was certain was Morris. As the second man turned it came as no surprise to see Morris himself.

Chapter Twenty-Two

I turned to the Professor, asking quietly, 'What should we do, Professor?'

He thought for a moment but a fleeting glance in Ruthie's direction quickly made up his mind.

'We shall reveal ourselves, William. We must enlist their help for Ruthie. Get her back to the basement. Myself and Professor Doolan will have much to discuss afterwards, I am certain of it.'

As relieved as I was at the prospect of getting Ruthie home, I felt a pang of nervousness at showing myself to Morris and his companion. Something of their bearing did not fill me with confidence. As I rose from my position I could hear a strange sound. It was nothing I'd ever heard before and I looked about curiously for a moment. I thought I would have been spotted straight away, but then I realised the men were distracted by something on the other side of the promontory.

As a group, we once more hefted Ruthie into the air and began the final leg over the loose rocks and pebbles that lie between us and the Gateway. As we neared and the sound of the rocks being disturbed by our unsteady progress was finally heard, Morris and his cohort turned in our direction.

'Who's there?' Morris called out, moving towards us.

As he made out our faces I saw recognition dawn. His eyes widened.

'It's me, William, and I'm with the Professor and Ruthie. She's hurt, badly. We need to get her back through the gateway,' I shouted urgently, hoping that any conflict over what had happened to the gate would be put to one side.

As we came closer he looked down at the stretcher before calling to his companion.

'Henry, go get the Professor, now!' He said. 'Put her down.' He refused to move out of our way as the other man walked into the Gateway, pausing for a second to pull on a pair of goggles of his own.

I stared at Morris in frustration, growing angry as he blocked our way.

'Out of our way!' Demanded Professor Thorebourne, stepping forward as if to brush him aside.

'We'll wait for Professor Doolan, if it's all the same to you, Sir.'

'It most certainly is not!' The Professor straightened himself in a most indignant manner, appearing shocked at how belligerent Morris appeared.

Just as I thought the Professor was about to wrangle with Professor Doolan's man, Professor Doolan himself stepped through the gateway closely followed by Henry, who looked a little uneasy at having to pass through the unfamiliar contraption.

'Ruthie, where's Ruthie?' Professor Doolan asked, before finding her lying on the makeshift stretcher before him. 'What happened? What have you done?'

'Done? We have done nothing at all. Ruthie followed us through and fell amidst the rocks. If you had not closed the gate behind us we would have had her safely home,' Professor Thorebourne looked quite apoplectic in his rage. 'I demand you explain yourself. What right have you to come to my home and interfere with my experiments?'

'She's ... She's not breathing.' We all stopped to look down at Ruthie then as her father leaned closer, searching for signs of life. 'She's dead. You've killed my daughter, you madman!'

'How dare y—' Professor Doolan rose up and launched himself at Professor Thorebourne before he could finish his sentence.

It all seemed to be happening in a strange dream to me. I barely saw the two Professor's fall to the ground as they began to wrestle with each other, so engrossed was I in looking upon Ruthie's face. I bent down slowly, touching her cheek and knowing from the coldness of her flesh that it was true. Ruthie had died even as we'd tried to get her to safety. In truth I cannot say with any certainty whether she would have lived if we'd had recourse to the Gateway immediately after her fall, but it did nothing to lesson the overwhelming guilt and grief that seemed to fall down upon me.

I became aware of an increasing intensity to the conflict and turned to see that our whaling friends were now trying to break up the fight. Before I knew what was happening Morris had produced a pistol from inside of his coat and was pointing it at

116

the whalers.

'STAND BACK!' He shouted fiercely.

Everything stopped then. Even the two Professor's became aware of something else happening above them and ceased their wrestling.

'Morris, what are you doing?' I asked, bewildered by what was taking place around me.

Professor Doolan refocused his attentions upon his daughter and crawled over to her, one eye darkening where he'd received a blow amidst the struggle. His grief came upon him then and he wept openly as he held her. I wanted to do the same, but I knew he would not allow that. Not now.

'This is your doing,' he shouted. 'I should leave you here, stranded. You deserve little else.'

'Let us take Ruthie back, Professor. Please?' I asked, just wanting to be away from this bleak place.

The unusual sounds I'd heard a short while earlier were still there, and I saw Henry move away to look down beyond the promontory. I couldn't help myself and I staggered across the loose surface, close to where the man was surveying the scene beyond. At first I saw nothing except more large boulders. Then I noticed them moving, and saw yet more in the water along the shoreline. I gazed out across the writhing mass before me, these elephantine animals with oversized tusks hanging from their mouths as they barked and howled, creating an unearthly sound in the fading light.

'Walrus,' said one of the whalers from behind me.

'I know. I saw one once at the zoo. There's so many of them.'

117

'Yeah, and they're hauling out too.'

'They're what?'

'Hauling out. They're gathering together on the beach. They do it every year, 'undreds of 'em.'

Even from this distance their size was impressive. Quite intimidating in fact. I wondered just how safe we were from them, whether they would attack us as intruders in their domain, or even as a potential meal. I held my tongue though, seeing Henry scowling over his shoulder.

'We should all get back through the Gateway. Don't you think?' I asked no one in particular.

The Gate itself seemed to glow ever brighter now that the sun had set. It was a clear night. The moon was up and shining brightly too, yet there was no competing with the Gateway's unnatural light.

I became aware of Professor Doolan's voice, cracking with grief as he threw his accusations at my mentor and guardian. Professor Thorebourne looked sad, but his eyes shone with his own accusations as he spoke.

'You tried to steal my work. It was your doing that Ruthie was here at all, Percival. How dare you blame me for this. I did not ask her here. I did not *want* her here.'

These last words seemed to stab me like a knife as I felt the shame of betraying his confidence and the guilt of not protecting her.

'Please, help me?' I asked in the direction of the three whalers that had congregated to one side, shielding their eyes against the Gateway's light. 'We need to take her back.'

'Through there?' Asked one, taking a small step back.

'Yes. It's the only way. It's quite safe, I assure you.' I could tell by their looks that they were unconvinced.

'It's bright,' said one.

'Oh, yes, sorry. I'll go through and find some eye protection,' I offered, glancing at the two Professor's as they continued to confront each other over Ruthie's lifeless body. Her father had draped a scarf over her face, but it did nothing to hide her from me.

Feeling myself becoming quite distraught by the whole affair, I brushed passed Morris and practically ran through the Gateway. I fancied I heard a shout following me through, as they realised where I was going. The familiar pull and push of the Gate was an almost reassuring sensation this time as I stumbled into the basement.

There was a sense of unfamiliarity for a moment as I looked around, seeing the signs of Professor Doolan and his men having been there. It looked as if they were prepared to carry things away in crates and I wondered just how long they would have dallied through the Gateway had we not come upon them. I didn't understand how another supposedly learned man from the Science Association could act in such an unethical manner. The basement was frigid. The increasing cold emanating from the Gateway was taking its effect and I could see a layer of frost developing upon the floor.

'Goggles!' I reminded myself, trying to ignore the angry shouts coming through the Gate. They were muffled enough that I could barely make out the words, but it was clear that the two Professor's were having at each other.

I rushed about in search of more goggles but only found one

other pair. It would have to do. We'd have to swap around as needed, at least, we would have done if there was any sense of cooperation between the two groups.

Turning back to the Gateway I took a deep breath and headed back for Ruthie, hoping that all of this could come to an end and we could bring Ruthie home. The question of what would be said of her untimely death struck me, but I put this to the back of my mind as my heart missed a beat at the thought of her. I don't think the events had really settled into my mind at this stage, as I sought to bring an end to this most traumatic of incidents. I'd no idea that events were about to become even worse than they already were.

Chapter Twenty-Three

Feeling myself pushed from the Gateway, I steadied myself on the other side and looked around. To my dismay the conflict between the two Professors seemed to be at its height as they each threw allegations at each other. Professor Thorebourne appeared thoroughly frustrated by his opponents behaviour and was of the opinion (quite rightly in my view) that he was in fact the one that had been ill-treated.

I was about to speak, to ask for the whalers help in taking Ruthie through when a hand grasped my upper arm and pulled me aside, thrusting me away from the Gate. I spun around to see Morris' angry eyes upon me.

'Don't try that again, Master Winn,' he said. 'I wouldn't want to have to hurt you now, Sir.'

The politeness mixed with an undoubted threat befuddled me for a moment and I looked back at him in confusion.

'You're staying here. Both of you!' He finished, his hand holding out the pistol.

I recoiled with fear, wondering why he was threatening me so. A sudden movement besides me drew my attention and I saw Thomas draw a long bladed knife from his belt, holding it out in front of him just as his friends pulled weapons of their own. The situation was swiftly turning ugly and dangerous.

'Yes, quite right, Morris,' said Professor Doolan, watching Morris as a strange calmness overcame his features. 'Henry will help me take my daughter through first.'

Henry seemed to hear his name all of a sudden and rushed to the Professor's side. I was still trying to fathom quite what was happening when the man lost his footing and slipped headlong into Morris. The whalers took their opportunity to disarm the man and lunged forward. What followed was a chaotic melee of bodies. I saw the flash of a knife and just as I was about to intervene, to instill some kind of order if that were possible, Morris's gun went off. The sharp report of the pistol took me by surprise. I stopped sharply as the men began to separate. I couldn't believe what I was seeing. What had become of our expedition.

Morris lay sprawled upon the ground, blood seeping through his clothes and onto the ground. He'd been stabbed in the belly and he didn't look good. Laurence, one of the whalers was also on the ground, but he was undoubtedly dead. The bullet had taken him in the chest and he'd fallen back onto the slope, coming to rest in a most awkward looking position.

No one spoke at this time as we all seemed to contemplate each other. The only sound was that of the nearby Walrus colony, raised up in its ire at the sudden intrusion of humans and the unexpected sound of gunfire. If ever an animal could sound angered or even outraged, then this was it.

'We must end this and get these men some help. Get everyone back through the Gateway, now,' I said in a far more assertive manner than I was feeling.

'Yes, Yes indeed,' agreed Professor Thorebourne, looking even more shocked by the turn of events than I felt.

The two Professors glared at each other for a moment, but the pained cries of Morris seemed to catch their attention and I could see sense returning to them once more.

'Yes, indeed,' said Professor Doolan, breaking any remaining stand off.

It seemed clear that we could do little for the whaler, but Morris was still alive and we owed these other men some succour from their troubles. Troubles that we had manifested upon them so unfairly.

I have to confess, I felt little sympathy for Morris's plight at this time. My heart was hardened given his treachery and the violence that he had inflicted, all in the course of trying to secure the Gateway's knowledge for Professor Doolan.

As a result I first tended to Ruthie. At first, Professor Doolan seemed intent upon stopping me from touching her, but as he gazed down upon her face, he stepped back in a sign that he simply wanted her away from here. Henry helped me, although no words passed between us. We hefted her up between us and with me leading the way we took her into the light. Once again I felt the pull-push of the Gateway, and for a moment I felt it almost pulling Ruthie away from me as I stepped through before the rest of her appeared, closely followed by Henry.

'We'll have to lay her on the floor. Gently, please,' I said, my grief surging through me as I looked on her unflinching countenance. I took a moment to cover her face before gesturing for Henry to go back through ahead of me. I had no intention of leaving him alone in the basement.

Next was the whaler. I had to pull my goggles away from my eyes to see in the darkness on the other side before I approached the two men that were huddled around their friend's body. I took his arm, indicating for his friends to help me in transferring him to the relative peace of the basement beyond the light. They both looked anxious over passing through the Gate, but I assured them all would be well as I steadied my grip on their fallen friend's arm. They took the proffered goggles for their protection and quickly drew them down against the light, before all three of us lifted the man between us.

The footing was loose and somewhat precarious, particularly with the weight of the man held between us. We stumbled and staggered toward the gate in what I can only deem a rather undignified manner. The men hesitated once more before entering through the brightness, but an encouraging nod of my head was enough to spur them on further.

As I stepped through the Gate I felt it pull me through, but as I was disgorged onto the other side it felt as though the man I was holding was almost being pulled apart. The Gateway wasn't quite wide enough for two men to walk through side by side, and so myself and the whaler holding his friend's other arm, sidestepped awkwardly through the space. For several seconds I was caught in-between the two locations and the sensations I was experiencing were rather disquieting. I was glad to find myself wholly on the other side, in the basement, as the whaler fumbled his way through, a half step behind. We hurried to pull the body through and for one highly disconcerting moment I had a vision of him being separated into two, leaving us holding onto just the top half of his body. My fears were unfounded and much to my relief the rest of him appeared with the other man still holding his legs.

Both whalers looked about themselves with an expression of awe. It was as if they'd never set eyes upon the basement of a house before. We laid the body down at the side of the gate, covering him with a sheet that I found nearby.

'I'll go back for the others,' I said, then a thought struck me. 'If it's not asking too much, would you be kind enough to ensure that both the Professor and I are in the basement before anyone is able to shut down the Gate?'

Thomas fixed me with an emotionless gaze, 'We will,' he said, and I knew from the hard edge to his voice that he'd have no intention of allowing Professor Doolan or his men to strand us once more.

A sound from the other side of the gate took my attention. It was certainly the roar of the walrus beyond, but it sounded close. I took a deep breath and hurried back through, determined to get Professor Thorebourne safely back into the basement.

Chapter Twenty-Four

As soon as I stepped out onto the stony ground beyond the Gateway I knew something was wrong. Even before I heard the threatening snorts and cries of the beasts I could sense that the situation had turned even more precarious.

Morris was still lying on the ground, but Professor Doolan was attempting to heave him up to his feet with Henry on his other side. Both men were looking elsewhere, their anxious expressions fixed upon the top of the slope where I could see several dark shadows lumbering towards us.

I spun around to find Professor Thorebourne and saw him nervously holding the pistol that Morris had used upon the whaler.

'Professor, we must go now!' I barked at him, trying to shake him from his paralysis. 'Professor!'

'Y-Yes, my boy?' He blinked several times before turning toward me. 'Oh, yes, indeed. I suppose we should.'

I stumbled over to him, being careful not to place myself

between the pistol and the oncoming beasts, I grasped his shoulder and began to pull him to the Gate. Professor Doolan was still struggling to get Morris to his feet who seemed to have turned into a dead weight in their hands. His cries of pain the only sign of him still being alive.

'I'll come back,' I called to them as I pushed the Professor ahead of me. He seemed to realise he was holding the weapon and threw it away from him just before he entered the gate, as if the idea of holding such a thing was entirely abhorrent.

I must have pushed him harder than I realised. As the pull and push of the Gate's forces disgorged us out of the other side we fell on top of each other. We landed in a messy tangle of arms and legs and I saw the two whalers look up from their dead friend, looking mildly surprised by our sudden appearance.

'The ... The Walrus',' I managed to hiss as I forced air back into my lungs having landed awkwardly.

'Aye, they'll be mad alright. Not the season t'be messing with 'em,' said Thomas.

For a moment I thought of not going back through. Of shutting down the gate and leaving Professor Doolan and his men stranded as they had done to us, but I knew I'd never forgive myself for such a cold act. The Professor pulled himself up into a sitting position, looking a little bewildered by everything that was going on. Satisfied that he was now safe, I stood up, brushing myself off before once more venturing through.

I'd barely placed my foot into the light when I felt something hit me, then I was being bundled to the floor as Henry fell backwards onto me, Morris' head and shoulders coming through with him.

'Move!' He shouted, staggering to his knees and pulling his friend through as best he could.

It took me another moment to recover. I was about to lend my own strength to his struggles when Thomas appeared at my shoulder and bent to take hold of the man. Between him and Henry they hauled Morris through inch by inch. I was sure I witnessed a stretching effect taking place as Morris lay half in and half out of the light. I stared at where his torso seemed to become elongated for a split second before he was pulled all of the way out, Professor Doolan following with a tenuous grasp of the man's ankles. He glanced behind him as he came, a look of panic in his eyes.

He'd barely cleared the light when the most astonishing sight I'd ever seen was presented to me. The seemingly outsized tusked head of a Walrus popped out of the Gateway. It gave out such a terrific bellow of anger that I stumbled back away from the Gate, coming up hard against the control panel. It bobbed its head as if trying to focus on this new world beyond the blinding light that it had thrust itself through, and began shuffling forwards, bending toward where Morris was prone on the ground as if to sniff out its opponent.

I saw Thomas grab a nearby spanner and quite recklessly take a swing at the beast. It glanced off its blubberous neck and the beast itself now focused upon him, pulling back for a moment before once more thrusting itself forwards. The Gate was not wide enough to take such an animal's girth, and I watched as it became wedged between the frame. I saw again the stretching effect that took place in its body and knew then that it was in pain. This only seemed to make it angrier as it struggled against the portal's opening, trying to force its way through and attack what it saw as the source of its distress.

To my horror I saw the entire Gateway move. The power of

the animal was such that it could not withstand such forces, and I saw sparks fly from the Gateway as its workings were assaulted.

'Shut it down! Shut it down now!' Cried the Professor, scrabbling away from the beast as best he could.

I turned around to the panel and looked for the switch to shut down the power. As I reached for it the Walrus bellowed once more and came crashing forward, causing some kind of power surge back through the circuits. The control panel sparked, before a blinding flash lit up the basement and smoke began to pour forth. By the time I was able to reach the switch it was too late. The circuits had fused (something I only later found to be the case) and I could do nothing to stop it.

'The engine, William, go to the engine and shut it down from inside the barn,' called the Professor.

'Yes, yes I will.'

I was in a flummox by this time. The enraged roars of the beast combined with the violent shaking of the Gate and the sparking, smoking controls in front of me was making clear thought almost impossible. I looked up to where the communication tunnel led from the basement and forced my legs into action. I looked around briefly as I reached the tunnel entrance, seeing Henry and the whalers trying desperately to keep the beast at bay with anything that came to hand. The two Professor's were both on the floor, their fearful expressions fixed upon the Gateway in horror.

Forgetting the low aspect of the tunnel, I caught myself a heavy blow as I raced into it and headed for our very own Beast. My head swam but I knew I had to get to the engine and disengage the power output without delay.

I'd reached the mouth of the tunnel with some relief. I tried blocking out the frightening sounds emanating from the basement, following upon my heels as I fled through the tunnel. I was beginning to think I'd reach the engine in time, when I felt something hit me from behind. The shockwave from the explosion threw me aside like a ragdoll, smoke and debris billowed from the mouth of the tunnel and for a while I was unable to think of anything much at all. There was something strange about that blast. It was the electromagnetic field that I supposed was behind it. It was as if the air itself were electrified around me. I felt my skin tingling and my hair standing up. My heart seemed to miss several beats and I was quickly engulfed by darkness.

Chapter Twenty-Five

As I slowly came to my senses I was aware of a deafening sound all about me. It took me some time to clear my head and realise the engine was still running in the barn. I'd ran from the basement without my ear dampeners and now I was being assaulted by the ear splitting sounds of the engine running out of control.

I pushed several pieces of debris from on top of me, trying to recall quite what had happened, but the engine's noise was making it difficult to think rationally. It took some effort to force myself to my feet. The barn was full of smoke and I had to feel my way through it to locate the controls. My head pounded and my ears buzzed as I tried to think of what to do. Eventually I managed to disengage the power, before pulling myself along the length of the engine on the steel rail that surrounded its platform to finish the job.

The vibrations in the floor began to lesson and I could feel some semblance of rational thought returning. I stood there for a while, catching my breath and checking myself for injury as I tried to imagine just what had happened inside of the basement after I'd left. The Walrus had damaged the Gateway, I knew that much, shorting out the controls somehow. I'd narrowly missed being caught in the blast that followed, the same could not be said of the others.

With a growing sense of trepidation, I started back toward the tunnel. The smoke lingered inside, making it difficult to see what lay ahead. As I began to make my way down into the darkness I was aware of just how quiet it was. The smoke would dampen most sounds, but an eery feeling of stillness seemed to leech out toward me as I trampled through the debris. I saw pieces of metal and wiring as I went, and then, lying beneath a stray piece of metalwork that was jammed across the tunnel, I saw a man's arm. As my eyes tracked along the torn flesh, passing over the scorched remains of the sleeve that still partially clung to it, any hopes of seeing a person on the other end were soon dashed. I felt sick to my very core and fought against my desire to vomit right there. This was not what was supposed to have happened. This was not what the Professor had worked so hard to achieve.

I was tempted to call out, to see if anyone would answer from inside the basement, but somehow I knew there was no one left to do so. My insides roiled the closer to the aftermath I came. I wanted to stop, to turn around and leave - never to return, but I knew I could not.

I picked my way through the debris, the smoke cloying at the back of my throat and causing me to retch. I fancied I could smell burnt flesh too, but I tried not to think too much upon this. I had to force my way passed the remains of the control panel and what appeared to be part of the Gateway's framework to finally reach the basement. What greeted me was something that will haunt me to the end of my days.

No one moved in that scorched ruination that was once the basement. The home of the Professor's most ambitious of projects. I puzzled over what lay amidst the jumble of machinery and wiring, before realising it was a mixture of human and Walrus remains.

I remember little of what happened next, other than falling to the floor in despair. I'd lost the Professor. I'd lost Ruthie. Other men had died there too, and the Gateway was utterly destroyed. I'd lost everything.

My mind fought to regain some momentum. To think of what to do next, but I drew a blank. I think I shut down then, both mentally and physically. I don't know how or when I left that basement. That place of utter despair, but I came to my senses as I sat in the drawing room and knew there was only one thing to do. There was only one man I felt I could call upon to help now.

As I think back now, I am surprised that our closest neighbours did not rush to find what had happened, but looking back, I don't think there was a great deal to show that anything on such a scale of death and destruction had come to pass. It would not be the first time the Professor had caused an unexpected explosion, but I'm sad to say it was the last.

Chapter Twenty-Six

'I'm sorry, George. It's not very pleasant down there,' I said, standing at the top of the basement stairs with George and his boys.

'Not to worry, Master Winn. We'll manage.' He looked uncertain for a moment. ''ave you thought of what to do wiv the ... um, bodies, Sir?'

'I ... I thought of the Professor's coffin. The one that he has in the potting shed. It's quite large in fact. I wonder if we might be able to transport it to St Pancras Church. I believe the Professor's sister is buried there.'

'I'm sure we can, Master Winn, although I don't know what the authorities will make of all of this. You say that there's those three whalers down there too? And an animal of some kind?'

'Yes, a Walrus of all things.'

'Never seen me one o' them before.'

'Do you think we could do this without the authorities really knowing? I mean, I don't quite know how I'd explain any of this. They're just as likely to think that I was the cause and that I'm creating a work of fiction to cover myself.'

George looked at me in such a way as I thought for a moment that was precisely what he believed, before saying, 'If I 'adn't 'ave seen the Professor's inventing meself, I might 'ave thought the same, I suppose.' He screwed his face up in concentration, before letting out a long breath. 'I suppose we could arrange something discreet, as it were. 'Specially as it's you, Master Winn. I'm sure the Professor wouldn't want you getting into any trouble on 'is account.'

'No, quite,' I answered quietly, feeling the grief building within at the thought of him and Ruthie.

Her and her father would be missed too, of course. I was at a loss as to know the best thing to do, but a quiet burial seemed the best thing all round to tell the truth.

Heading back into the basement proved to be a harrowing affair. George and his boys handled it with decorum, and despite the unpleasant nature of it all, they were able to clear the basement of debris and help me to gather up the sparse remains of those lost souls.

With their help I was able to move the coffin from the potting shed and into the house, where we were able to place the Professor, Ruthie and the rest inside. The Walrus remains proved difficult to handle, given the size of it and the rather unpleasant nature of its blubbery body. I couldn't help but think that the whalers would have taken such a thing in their stride.

It took all four of us to lift the largest part of the animal's body into the coffin, and around it we arranged the others. I didn't offer any explanation as to the three sacks that were already present in the coffin containing the heads, and George in his inimitable way never asked, although I caught a raised

135

eyebrow from him as he stared down at them. I'm not sure that he realised quite what was contained within.

The coffin was eventually manhandled out of the house and onto George's cart. We covered the coffin carefully in order to hide its outline, before we set off across London. It was a journey of utter sadness and remorse for my part, and I've no doubt George and his boys shared some of my grief. We encountered no problems on that final expedition, as I came to think of it, in the Professor's honour.

I'd arranged - with George's help, the services of the local priest, and we arrived at St Pancras church yard with little in the way of ceremony. We'd told him that it was another death from Typhoid, as at that time London was unfortunate enough to be in the grip of such an epidemic. Many were laid to rest there with little pomp or ceremony, and our burial was no different to many in most respects.

As I watched the coffin being lowered into the ground, I found myself at a complete loss as to what to do with myself. I'd never felt myself to be of the Professor's calibre in order to follow a life in science, but I felt I owed him enough to at least keep some involvement in the pursuit of knowledge.

There was very little conversation on the journey West, and I'm sad to say I saw very little of George and his boys from that day forth. I wonder sometimes if I did the right thing. If I should have in some way attempted to carry on the Professor's work, but his notes perished in the explosion and I have grave doubts as to whether any other would have the vision that Professor Thorebourne had for such things.

I content myself with the idea that an Interspacial Gateway, such as it was, would only have brought destruction upon the world, as I've little doubt that great nations would come to war over such a great possession and the power that it could bring. I suppose it's just as well that it is no more, but I'll never forget the time that I stepped through the world's first and only Interspacial Gateway, and survived to tell the tale. The only living person to have done so.

Many thanks for reading!

If you enjoyed my book it would be great if you could leave a review.

For updates on new and future releases please visit my website and sign up to my free mailing list:

https://mfindlaywriter.wordpress.com

You can also follow me on:

Facebook: @MFindlay.Writer

Or

Twitter: @MFindlay_Writer

Coming Soon...

VICTORIA
and the
TIME
TRAVELLER

A Victorian Steampunk adventure
based on a true event

M Findlay

About the author

Born in London, England. The author spent many years working in computing, and in particular as a software developer. They've also experienced life as a nurse, in animal care, and having joined the Royal Navy upon leaving school - soon discovered that following orders was not their strong point!

Having moved away from computing and spending several years writing under other names and in different genres, they're now embracing their true love for Science Fiction and Fantasy writing.

Imagining the future development of mankind and its many possibilities is something that's held a fascination from a young age, and so too has the idea of creating entirely new worlds and cultures.

From the author:

As the great Arthur C. Clarke once said:

"..science fiction is something that could happen – but usually you wouldn't want it to. Fantasy is something that couldn't happen – though often you only wish that it could."

I hope that you enjoy reading my books just as much as I've enjoyed writing them!

Printed in Great Britain
by Amazon

35824815R00081